Cover Copy

Lilias adores the depths of the sea, but when scales form on her legs, she discovers she's Changing. Becoming something else. Something otherworldly. The top half of her body is still human, but her lower half is now morphing into that of a fish and soon, she'll no longer be able to walk on land. In all her eight-hundred years, nothing like this has ever happened to her or any of her fellow water fae. She needs answers—and to find the eldest of her fae kind who's gone missing—except it seems there is only one man who can aid her in her mission. His name is Levi Matheson, and he's a fae-blooded shifter from a time far in the future.

Never has Levi met a more maddening, stunning…um, woman/mermaid like Lilias? Intent on aiding her in her mission, he is sent hurtling across the realms with her. She's evolving right before his eyes, and he's running out of time. What's worse? He's also one-hundred percent certain she's his fated mate. Which leaves one gaping problem. How on earth does he complete the bond with her when she has a tail?

Highlander's Mermaid is the magical retelling of the merpeople—an ancient race born to live in the sea. If you love fantasy, adventure, and romance, then don't miss this enchanting tale.

Books by Joanne Wadsworth

The Matheson Brothers Series
Highlander's Desire, Book 1
Highlander's Passion, Book 2
Highlander's Seduction, Book 3
Highlander's Kiss, Book 4
Highlander's Heart, Book 5
Highlander's Sword, Book 6
Highlander's Bride, Book 7
Highlander's Caress, Book 8
Highlander's Touch, Book 9
Highlander's Shifter, Book 10
Highlander's Claim, Book 11
Highlander's Courage, Book 12
Highlander's Mermaid, Book 13

Highlander Heat Series
Highlander's Castle, Book 1
Highlander's Magic, Book 2
Highlander's Charm, Book 3
Highlander's Guardian, Book 4
Highlander's Faerie, Book 5
Highlander's Champion, Book 6
Highlander's Captive, Novella 0.5

Princesses of Myth Series
Protector, Book 1
Warrior, Book 2
Hunter, Novella 2.5
Enchanter, Book 3
Healer, Book 4
Chaser, Book 5

Books by Joanne Wadsworth

Regency Brides Series
The Duke's Bride, Book 1
The Earl's Bride, Book 2
The Wartime Bride, Book 3
The Earl's Secret Bride, Book 4
The Prince's Bride, Book 5
Her Pirate Prince, Book 6

Sweet Regency Tales
(Sweet/tame version of Regency Brides)
The Duke Who Stole My Heart, Book 1
The Earl I Adore, Book 2
To Love During War, Book 3
My Secret and the Earl, Book 4
The Prince Who Captured Me, Book 5
Beware of the Pirate Prince, Book 6

Billionaire Bodyguards Series
Billionaire Bodyguard Attraction, Book 1
Billionaire Bodyguard Boss, Book 2
Billionaire Bodyguard Fling, Book 3

Highlander's Mermaid

The Matheson Brothers, Book 13

JOANNE WADSWORTH

The Legend

In the twelfth century, a man named Gilleoin became the first and only known man to hold bear shifter blood, an ability gifted to him by The Most High One. His clan was called Matheson, and when he mated with a woman carrying faerie blood, they created a line shrouded in secrecy, a line guarded by the immortal fae princess, Cherub. Through the endless streams of time, she will be there for them, never forsaking her people, either in the present or far into the past.

Atlantis

Many thousands of years in the past, Poseidon took a beautiful human woman named Cleito as his lover. Cleito gave birth to five sets of twin sons, the eldest known as Atlas. Poseidon created the land known as Atlantis and built a sanctuary for Cleito on the hilltop in the center of the land and surrounded it with circular bands of water and land. When Atlas came of age, Poseidon appointed him as King of Atlantis.

The son Poseidon had from his marriage to Amphitrite named Triton, held the upper body of a man and the lower body of a fish. Triton could swim within the seas or take land legs and walk upon the Earth. He coveted all that Atlas ruled, and it wasn't long before bitterness began to brew in Triton's heart, his anger growing toward his father and his half-brother. He decided he would take Atlantis from Atlas, except Poseidon learned of his intent and was furious. For his act of treachery, Poseidon punished Triton by locking his land legs away for the next one-hundred years.

Triton fought the punishment handed down to him by Poseidon by discovering a way to circumvent his sentence. It appeared he could outwit his father by transferring the curse to another of his tailed kind, provided he could capture their tears and never spill them. Unfortunately, his race of merpeople now neared extinction, their numbers dwindling. His race's women, known as the Sirens of the Sea, had chosen to separate themselves from the mermen, who sought only to mate with the sirens and get them with child, before abandoning them. The sirens preferred to take human lovers, men who would raise their children with them, so they sought sanctuary beyond Atlantis in the human realm.

Triton had no intention of transferring his curse to one of his fellow mermen. There were only a handful of them remaining, so he was left with only one choice, he would create a new race of merpeople by kidnapping the eldest of the water fae, a woman named Breena, who could already breathe below the surface of the sea. He would force a tail upon her. He was a sorcerer, could weave such spells with ease. Except he'd have to be cleverer than the water fae. They would fight his edict, but he had no intention of allowing them to halt his coming rule. He would create his very own new race and reign over them.

The Seer – Murdock Matheson

Matheson Castle, led by Murdock Matheson, the Chief of Clan Matheson, a man with dual fae-shifter blood, Scotland, current day.

Murdock Matheson jerked upright in bed, fists clenched in his brown fur covers, his chamber on the upper floor of the castle as dark as the darkest of nights. Not an ember glowed in his fireplace and not a trickle of moonlight shimmered through his open window. Aye, the skies beyond were obliterated by heavy black clouds, so thick and daunting, the same as the heavy cloud of unease which had jolted him from his sleep.

In the past, whenever he had awoken this abruptly from his rest, his seer ability would rise forth and now was no exception. With his focus on his second sight, a vision slammed forth to full life, his psychic senses taken by a barrage of images.

Standing on the sandy curve of a loch, a crowd of perhaps thirty stared out in utter silence at the shimmering waves rolling into shore, their arms linked. The waning sun shone through the heavy cloud cover with spears of golden light that bathed the darkening waters a liquid golden hue.

The crowd drew tighter together, their bare feet sinking into the sand as they formed a protective half circle around one woman wearing a white silken gown with silver braided sashes belted at her waist, her gaze cast out over the dark waters of the loch. Lilias. Murdock would never mistake her. She was an immortal, one of the ancient fae, a being of over eight-hundred years of age, her two identical sisters having recently accepted the bond with two of his clansmen. She was one of the water fae and could control the element of water, could swim easily within the chilly depths of the ocean. With her red hair falling in waves to the small of her lower back, she tipped her face up to the skies as the light of the day slowly disappeared and night took firm hold.

The nighttime wind rose, whistling about her.

Lilias removed the braided sash at her waist and allowed the tasseled belt to slither into a silvery pool on the fine white grains at her feet. Slowly, she lifted the hem of her gown to her knees…and Murdock caught his breath.

A patchy smattering of pearl-colored scales glittered on her calves.

How unusual. Murdock had never seen such a thing. The water fae didn't have scales.

Lilias breathed deep, squeezed her eyes tightly shut then opened them again before turning from the sea and facing the crowd. Voice raised, she said to everyone,

"These scales are proof that Triton means our water fae harm. He stole Breena from us and now we're all Changing, because of him." She swept a hand down her legs as a wave crashed into shore and hit the backs of her knees. The water retreated, leaving bubbles foaming at her bare feet, her scales wet and sparkling brighter.

"Why would Triton steal her away?" One of the surrounding women stepped forward, her hands clenched in her robes and the same smattering of pearl-colored scales visible on her calves.

"Triton is the son of Poseidon, the God of the Sea, and these scales are the mark of Triton's merpeople, a race currently nearing extinction. When I last spoke to Breena, she told me she'd come face to face with Triton within the waters near Atlantis, that he'd threatened her. He said he would soon rule over the water fae, and he meant it. Do you all remember, only a fortnight past, when Triton attempted to take Atlantis from King Atlas and failed? Poseidon was furious and punished Triton for his insurrection by locking his land legs away for the next one-hundred years, although word is, Triton can transfer the curse to another of his tailed kind if he captures their tears and never spills them. Breena summoned me here to this loch after her return. This is where we spoke, right here on this shore." Lilias glanced out over the water once more, despair etched across her face. "Breena thought it best to lock our gateway portal and ensure Triton couldnae enter our realm. She swam down to secure the portal's arch, but that is when the seabed shook, and our portal got buried under a mountain of rock and rubble. I'm certain Triton must have used his trident against us. He can strike the earth and cause disruption with it, and now, 'tis only a matter of time afore Triton breaks her."

"Where will he have taken her?" the same woman asked.

"I suspect somewhere within the chain of the Adonis Isles. 'Tis where Triton has his lair, although I dinnae know the exact location of it."

A man stepped forward and grasped Lilias's shoulders. "There are over three-hundred islands in that chain, more than six-hundred smaller islets, and dozens of atolls, all spread over six-thousand sea leagues. How are we supposed to find Breena when we no longer have a seabed portal to take us through time to her? Ours is buried."

"I've already enlisted Cherub and Cairstine's aid. They should be here any moment—"

A huge dragon soared above the treetops and roared, its golden-white scales glinting with a sizzling red glow as it sent fire streaming high into the sky from its massive jaws. It flapped its powerful wings and sent a blast of sand skittering across the beach. Murdock had seen that dragon many-a-time. It was Cairstine. She was Lilias's sister, older than her by a couple of minutes, the woman one of the ancient fae who could morph into any form she wished, her dragon one of her favorite entities.

Circling wide, Cairstine's dragon slowed its descent and landed with a mighty *thump* that shook the ground. The dragon spewed more fire which sizzled across the waves, while atop the dragon's neck, Cherub sat between two spiked barbs. As a time-walker, Cherub was the faerie king's eldest child, and could control the element of air, could open a portal, and travel back and forth through time as needed. The breeze fluttered the draping sleeves of

Cherub's regal burgundy gown, her long skirts swishing about her ankles as she rose into the air and floated down toward Lilias.

More fire blazed and the dragon morphed, the sparks slowly subsiding and revealing Cairstine clothed in a sapphire gown with sweeping skirts.

"Sorry for our delay. Your sister and I came as soon as we could, my dear niece." Cherub kissed Lilias's cheek. "Do you have any further information to hand?"

"Only that which I've already shared with you, that Triton has a lair somewhere within the Adonis Isles, that we must make all haste to find Breena." Lilias hugged Cairstine. "Sister, I cannae reach Breena telepathically, and I fear Triton has forged a spell over her to halt any connection we might try to make with her."

"I've tried to reach her too, been unable to make contact. I detest Triton, always have. His curse belongs to him and no one else. We will teach him that lesson soon enough." Blowing out a puff of smoke, Cairstine plucked between two teeth with one finger. "When we find him, I shall fry him then eat his ashes. Show me your scales, dear sister. I have no' yet seen them."

Lilias lifted the hem of her skirts, turned one calf toward Cairstine and her aunt, her scales glinting in the moonlight. "These are proof that Triton has already begun to Change the water fae. He intends on creating his very own new race of merpeople, with us as his slaves."

Cherub crouched and touched Lilias's scales. "'Tis no wonder the sirens abandoned their realm and prefer the human world. Triton is a menace." She eyed the crowd. "Do you all have these scales?"

"Aye, we do," they chorused.

"Well, it appears we cannae tarry a moment longer." Cherub waved one of the men forward. "Shaw, I shall open a portal and take Lilias and Cairstine with me to the Adonis Isles. While we're gone, you must do all you can to clear the rubble from the seabed portal. We need to know if our portal has survived the landslide intact."

"Princess, of course." Shaw gave Cherub a respectful bow.

Cherub stirred the wind with a swish of her hands and called out over the rising gale. "Step clear, everyone."

Shaw ushered the other water fae toward the sand dunes, and Cherub whisked the wind harder until a wild and windy vortex opened.

"Lilias, Cairstine, hurry and hold on to me now," Cherub shouted over the rush of wind. "Neither of you are allowed to let go while we're traveling, otherwise you'll experience a far rougher journey than what is necessary."

"Aye, we'll hold on to you tight." Lilias grabbed ahold of Cherub's right arm while Cairstine took Cherub's left. The wind tunneled around the three women and then within the blink of an eye, they got sucked away into the dark abyss.

Hell, Murdock needed to remain on full alert. He wished he could travel to the Adonis Isles with them, but since he couldn't, he'd maintain a close watch and ensure he spoke to Cherub if he had another vision.

Chapter 1

Stars whizzed by as Lilias traveled through Cherub's portal.

Lightning flashed and she gasped at the absolute beauty of moving through both time and space. More stars, the wind whipping her white silken skirts about her legs, her scales snagging the fine fabric about her calves. A cloying mist suddenly swirled all around and the lights flickered out. She held tight to Cherub's arm and made a grab for Cairstine's hand in the darkness, but an unearthly force suddenly sucked them all apart and she splashed into the sea. Went down, down, and down.

Kicking hard, she swam within the murky darkness and broke through to the surface as waves crashed all around. Cherub and Cairstine popped up a few feet distant and with another kick, she reached them. "Are you both all right?"

"Aye. Look there." Cherub stabbed a finger at the shore of one of the many islands within the Adonis Isles.

They'd traveled back many thousands of years. "See if you can reach Breena telepathically. We must try again, just to be sure about Triton's spell, that he indeed spoke one over her to halt any connection."

"I'll try." She sent her mind soaring outward but caught no trace of Breena. Sheer silence rebounded. "Nay, 'tis the same as afore. If we wish to find her, we will need to search these waters and the land until we discover Triton's lair. We have no other recourse."

"I'll take to the skies, search to the north and swing around to the south via the eastern horizon then continue in ever widening circles." Cairstine shoved her wet locks from her face. "Keep in contact."

"Of course, and Lilias and I will take this islet and then the opposite horizon to you." Cherub shimmered into her mist form and whisked upward and streamed toward the beach where the surf crashed along the sandy shoreline.

"Take care, dear sister." Lilias kicked toward land just as Cairstine morphed with a blaze of lights into her golden eagle form and heaved into the night sky. Her sister could shift shape into any form she chose, from the smallest insect to the largest of creatures.

Cairstine shook her feathers then morphed again into her dragon, her huge beast sending a backdraft of wind and water at her. Her sister glided in a circle overhead. Moonlight penetrated through the blackened clouds and shimmered over Cairstine's dragon's scales as she flew past the beach and disappeared into the distance.

Breathing deep, Lilias swam toward the cove, her night vision reversing the black depths of the sea to a brilliant emerald green. Anything that moved through that green would be visible. She spied a stingray and a school of fish with a baby shark nearing the school. She rarely intervened with nature below the surface, but her emotions were touchy this night, so she summoned her ability and flicked one hand at the shark before it opened its jaws on the fish. A wave of water knocked the shark off its course and the creature tumbled over, missing its intended victims. At least she'd saved some fish this night.

Remaining alert and kicking hard, she cut through the swell on a direct path toward the beach surrounded by sandstone cliffs that glowed a silvery-white hue under the moonlight.

She caught the crest of the next wave and rode the whitecaps into the bay.

The wave crashed into shore, and she tumbled through the surf and got dumped onto the wet sand. Oh, my goodness. Never had she had such an inelegant landing. Pushing to her feet, she faced the cliffs rising high either side of the bay and noted the pathway cutting into the cliff face which led upward and to the right, a jagged and uneven path but a clear one all the same. *"Cherub?"* She reached out to her aunt, who unfortunately didn't hold the same telepathic ability as Lilias and her sisters. *"Where are you?"*

"This islet is small, with barely any vegetation. Topside of that cliff is naught but a bay on the other side. We should continue our search elsewhere. There is naught here. I'll take us to the skies. I'm coming." Cherub materialized from her mist form in front of her, her white fur cloak flapping back from her shoulders, her gaze going to Lilias's feet. "Oh dear, when did that happen?"

"When did what happen?" She eyed her own feet just as something tickled her toes. She wriggled them in the sand and caught the sight of a thin webbing that had formed. "Well, that's new."

"The merpeople have webbing between their toes too." Cherub cast her a dismal look. "It appears you're transitioning even more into one of them."

"I'm going to kill Triton when we find him."

The tickling sensation intensified, and she lost her balance as sparks flared from her legs. She toppled back into the whitewash of bubbles and landed with a splash on her bottom, one very scaly bottom. She dug her elbows into the wet sand, got enough leverage and hauled the hem of her sodden gown to her thighs. A tail poked out, the tidal line of the sea flowing back and forth over the lower half of her body. She lifted her tail and dropped it with a splat, water and grains spraying everywhere. "Well, now all my fears have been realized. I look just like one of the sirens."

"Can you feel your legs at all?" Cherub asked as she dropped to her knees on the sand beside her. Gently, her aunt touched her scaly tail and blew out a long shuddering breath before poking and prodding the entire length of her new appendage. "Well, it isnae all that bad. 'Tis pretty at least."

"My legs feel as if they're there, except for the fact that they're not." She smoothed over the scales down to where her knees should be, could make out the curvature below the scales as she reflexively tried to draw her knees up, not that she got far. She could only bend her tail to a certain degree. Her new appendage wasn't as flexible as her legs. No crawling across the sand for her. She would be stuck with belly shuffling over the white grains until she became dry, or at least that was the case for the merpeople. Once dry, their tails shimmered away, their land legs reappearing. "Could you help me get to the sand dunes? I need to get farther from the water."

"Of course." Cherub hooked her arms under her arms and dragged her up higher onto the sand, then her aunt stirred the wind and it rose and breezed over her.

Lilias flapped the hem of her gown, the wind catching and fluttering her silken skirts about her tail. "Oh my, if I've got a tail then that means so do Shaw and the other water fae."

"Reach out to them and confirm." More wind from Cherub.

She sent her mind spinning out, tried to find Shaw but sensed he already spoke telepathically to another. "Drat it. He's busy. I'll try again later."

"Let's assume they have all forged tails, the same as you have." A firm nod from Cherub.

"'Tis a logical assumption since our scales appeared at the same time."

A seal suddenly barked and surged from the surf. No ordinary seal. The selkie named Oadh. Lilias would never mistake him with his distinctive black crescent-shaped mark adorning his gray and white speckled forehead. With a slap of his flippers, Oadh shuffled toward her, his flesh slick and shiny and his black eyes glittering under the moonlight. He rose onto his hind flippers, his beast twice her size, then out in the night-shrouded water, another seal streamed through the waves and belly-shuffled forward. Roy. He was Oadh's brother, the two of them inseparable.

Roy had an unmistakable notch in his right flipper, a notch he'd acquired in his youth when he'd gotten too close to a hungry shark.

"What are you two doing here?" The wind breezed over Lilias. "You're a long way from your selkie realm."

Oadh barked from deep within his creature then shook. The ground moved as layers of his dark skin rippled to his seal's hind flippers and pooled on the sand. Naked and heavily muscled, with impressively thick biceps and legs as large as tree trunks, Oadh clasped his hands behind his back and offered Cherub and her a respective bow, his shaved head gleaming under the moonlight and water running down his wide chest in long rivulets. "Our mother sent us."

"Did she have a vision?" The men's mother was the selkie seer, Aisling, an ancient and wise woman the fae respected.

"Aye. She can see both into the past and into the future, and she foresaw yer plight this night, is aware that Triton stole Breena away, that yer water fae have now forged tails. Her vision rang with strength. She asked us to pass on her words, said, 'If the water fae wish to find their kin, then ye must first locate the amulet once held by Ula, the eldest Siren of the Sea. The amulet will allow ye to open a portal directly to Breena and Triton so ye can rescue her.'"

"Ula lost her amulet eons ago." Lilias rolled onto her belly and heaved closer, Roy still in his seal form, the man rarely taking his human form since he was born mute and preferred his creature's skin.

"Do ye remember the strength of her amulet though?"

Oadh asked her.

"Aye, I remember that Triton was after it all those centuries ago, knew it held the power to open a water portal directly to the one the holder desired to see, that the holder needed only to speak that person's name and the amulet would take them to them by way of a whirlpool. I'm certain Ula was gifted the amulet by the Tuath Dé afore they left Earth for the Otherworld."

"Aye, she was, her relationship with the Tuath Dé one she treasured."

"Then how are we supposed to find her amulet when 'tis lost?"

"Ula never lost it. Aisling instructed her to place the amulet in a safe place in the human realm, to leave it there so Triton couldnae get his devious hands on it. Ula abided by her decree and hid it."

"So, all we need to do is find Ula if we wish to borrow her amulet?"

"One cannae find Ula, no' unless she wishes to be found. Aisling said the quickest path to finding Breena is by retrieving the amulet."

"How do we retrieve it if we dinnae know where it is, nor can ask Ula to tell us?"

"Aisling said ye would ask that, but to tell ye to speak to Ailith instead. Yer and Cairstine's eldest sister can see visions of war, and 'tis war that is coming for ye and yer fellow water fae. Only Ailith's visions will be able to guide ye the best."

"Then I shall speak to her." She dipped her head in thanks just as more wind rose, the last drops of water drying from her skin. Bright lights suddenly burst all around her. Her tail shimmered and disappeared, her land legs returning.

Oadh eyed her, his expression grave as she clambered to her feet. "Ye know Aisling speaks the truth. Will ye follow her advice?"

"Aye, we would be fools no' to." She grasped her aunt's hand, and Cherub nodded her agreement. Come hell or high water, she and her loved ones wouldn't rest until they'd found Ula's amulet and rescued Breena. Triton would regret the day he decided to take on the water fae.

Chapter 2

Matheson Castle, fortress of clan Matheson, current day.

On guard in the misty moonlight, Levi Matheson patrolled the battlements of Matheson Castle, his sword holstered at his side. Beyond the curtain wall, all remained eerily quiet, which made his inner bear claw under his skin.

Jaw clenched, he ducked into the gatehouse security control room, the screen showing the feed from the surveillance cameras mounted on the uppermost corners of the ramparts. Only the stillness of the night and nothing more flickered back at him. Nothing to worry about. No present danger. Except still, it wouldn't hurt to check the far perimeter before his shift ended.

He switched the feed to the camera kept high on a pole at the edge of the loch.

With a quick turn, he swiveled the camera in a full circle and scanned the dark, glassy waters of Loch Alsh, then rechecked the edge of the woods.

All appeared tranquil, which was quite at odds with how he felt.

Taking a deep breath, he calmed himself as moonlight shimmered over the forest stretching for miles upon miles into the mountainous ranges of the Highlands. Their fae-shifter clan needed the elevated level of isolation their stronghold provided from the rest of the world. It aided them in so many ways, giving them both the perfect level of security to keep their abilities concealed from others, and for their bears to roam the woods, in privacy, as needed.

"Anything to report before I take over?" Liam strode inside the control room and lazily dropped into the chair beside him, leaned back and crossed his arms behind his head. "Any dragons about tonight?"

"There's only one dragon and she's your mate. Thankfully, she took off with Cherub, although I don't know to exactly where. Can you offer any insight?"

"She and Cherub went to pick up Lilias from the fae realm then head on over to the Adonis Isles. I'd hoped she'd be back by now."

"The Adonis Isles, as in *The Adonis Isles* in the realm of Atlantis?" He'd heard Lilias speak of Atlantis a time or two, not that she visited the realm all that often. He raised a brow at Liam. "Did you take that fancy red pill of yours tonight, the one that makes you say strange things?"

"Those red pills help me to recover quicker from blood loss when Cairstine feeds from me. I crafted them myself, and they're filled with all sorts of healthy vitamins and minerals." Liam slapped his arm. "They've gone to the realm of Atlantis. You know Breena, right?"

"Aye, I've met her. She's the eldest of the water fae, one of Lilias's dearest friends."

"Well, I've got some sad news. Breena's gone missing, taken to the Adonis Isles by Triton."

"Are we talking about Triton, the son of Poseidon?"

"We are, and he prefers to remain in his own realm back in the time of Atlantis."

"Jeez, there is absolutely nothing normal about our clan anymore." Levi scratched his head. "When will we know if they've found Breena?"

"I'm not sure. My mated link with Cairstine is on the blitz with her so far away."

"Will Ailith know? I saw her and Hunter wander down to the loch half an hour ago. They disappeared into the woods but might have returned by now." Levi would go to Lilias's sister to get more information if needed.

"She might." Liam snagged his arm before he could leave the room. "Wait. There's one more thing I should tell you, something Lilias told Cairstine before my mate left Matheson Castle with Cherub this evening. The water fae have now got scales, and the reason why Triton's involved is because he intends on turning them into his own tailed kind. That's why he stole Breena. He wants to capture her tears, which will transfer his punishment to her. Punishment exacted on Triton by Poseidon after he tried to take the Kingdom of Atlantis away from King Atlas."

"Is Lilias in trouble?" Levi paced the room. It was no wonder he'd felt off this night, particularly if Lilias was in trouble. He'd always had a connection to her, ever since the moment they'd first met.

"I'm not sure. Speak to Ailith and ask her to get an

update." Liam tapped the surveillance screen. "She and Hunter have just emerged from the woods. They're down by the loch."

Levi checked the screen which showed Ailith crouching on the beach, one hand spread over the sand where the waves foamed up and slowly receded. "She must have sensed a vision with her skill."

"Get me an update on Cairstine while you're down there."

"I'm on it." He had no intention of remaining out of the loop a moment longer, not if something big was going on with Lilias.

He marched out the door, bounded down the stairs and ducked out the postern gate. He scanned the woods, his shifter sight alone allowing him to see exceptionally well in the gloomy dark, his bear still pricking under his skin. Jogging, he followed the trail down to the beach as the moon cast its silvery glow across the wispy streaks of fog clinging to the surface of the loch.

Ahead, Ailith and Hunter spoke in a hushed tone, Ailith dressed in her battle leathers and Hunter in camouflage cargo pants and a black shirt with daggers sheathed at his wrists. Ailith glanced at Levi, and he raised a hand in a wave as he joined them. "I've just finished my shift, was in the control room with Liam. What can you tell us about the situation with Lilias and the water fae?"

"I'm no' sure if what I've seen is good news or bad." Ailith scrubbed a hand across her face, worry creasing her brow. "Cairstine searches the skies over the Adonis Isles, while I've seen Lilias on the beach with a tail, and two selkies coming ashore."

"Who are the selkies?"

"Oadh and Roy. They were sent to Lilias by the selkie seer Aisling."

"The selkie have a seer?"

"Aye, and she had a message for Lilias. Oadh just passed it along."

"What did the seer say?"

"That Lilias must find Ula's amulet, an ancient Celtic charm that allows the holder to wish their way to whomever they desire by way of a whirlpool."

"Who's Ula?" He'd never heard Lilias mention Ula's name.

"Ula is the first Siren of the Sea, created by Poseidon for Triton, although Ula and her sister sirens no longer live in the realm of Atlantis, nor does Ula speak to Triton unless absolutely necessary. The sirens prefer to mate with human men. The sirens can use the seabed portals to travel across the centuries and the realms, and from what I've seen in my vision, Ula's amulet isnae lost as we've always believed, but is in fact hidden somewhere safe on Earth to keep it out of Triton's devious hands. 'Tis made of Celtic gold and has a large white pearl in the center, and in my vision, I saw it deep down beneath the water. Let me see if I can encourage another vision to arise." Ailith closed her eyes, dug her hand into the sand and went quiet. Long minutes passed before she finally spoke, her eyes still closed. "Oh my, I see you, Levi, and Lilias. The two of you are sitting on a boulder beside a pool of water somewhere in the mountains. Lilias has a tail, and the water is deep. It swirls afore you, as if a portal is being opened."

"A portal with the amulet?"

"I believe so." She opened her eyes. "My vision has come to an end, but I will keep a close eye out for further visions. For now, you and Lilias must stay together if Ula's amulet is to be recovered. Once you have the amulet, you must use it to find and rescue Breena. I wish I could see more, surely will in time."

"Then that's what we'll do. Lilias and I will remain together until we recover the amulet." He'd do anything for Lilias, cut out his heart if she asked him. "Can you reach Lilias for me?" All three sisters, Ailith, Cairstine, and Lilias, were telepaths and could speak mind to mind with each other, the women born within minutes of each other, triplets who were identical in every way.

"I'll try." She grasped his hands. "But first, you must give me your word you'll keep my youngest sister safe."

"You have my word." An easy oath to give.

Chapter 3

Royal Palace of the Fae, realm of the fae, the next morning.

Lilias plopped onto the lid of her wooden trunk under her bedchamber window after speaking with Ailith about the vision she'd had. Tracing one finger down the glass pane, she followed the trickle of falling raindrops from outside. Thunderclouds had brewed, a storm unleashed in the skies over the palace. Goodness, just one drop of rain would have her crashing onto the ground, her tail returning in a blaze of sparks. She didn't wish for that, or at least not again this morn. She rubbed her elbow where she'd already hit the floor mere moments after awakening. Washing the sleep from her eyes had been a terrible mistake, the water on her skin sending her careening to the floor.

"Princess." Shaw knocked on her open door then stepped back and pressed his hands behind his back, his billowy white tunic tucked loosely into his belted blue tartan kilt, his scales glittering on his calves.

"Good morn, Shaw. How are you this morn?"

"I'm well. I've called a meeting in the great hall for the water fae, so we might discuss the pitfalls we've learned since last eve when we forged our tails, of which my first lesson for you would be a warning. If you leave your finger on that windowpane for much longer, you'll soon be flapping about on the floor. The moisture can bead on the inside of the glass causing a Change."

"Oh, dear. You have my thanks for the warning." She pulled her finger back. "Although I cannae attend the meeting since I'm waiting for Cherub so I can return to Matheson Castle. Ailith had a vision last eve, one showing her that I need to work closely with Levi to find Ula's amulet. Apparently, Levi and I must stay together for the foreseeable future." She'd only learned of her sister's vision after retiring to her chamber late last eve. "How goes the unburying of our seabed portal? I'm eager to hear of any developing news."

"Devon has devised an underwater pulley system and has managed to clear several of the larger boulders. There is a great mountain of rocks to get through, so it could take some time. I expect five or six days. I'll be working closely with Devon and the water fae to uncover it, of course, with all speed." He tapped his chin. "There is an additional option to hasten the process that you might like to hear about."

"Aye, please tell me."

"When I spoke to Cherub last eve, she was pondering an idea, wondering if she could open one of her own portals from the safety of the shore of Loch Heart all the way down to the debris covering our seabed portal. Her thought was if she could stir the wind strong enough within one of her portals, she might be able to cause enough strength and velocity within the water to whip the smaller rocks into the funnel and suck them up to the shore. All we'd need to do was to remove the larger rocks first, those which would never move or transport through her portal."

"For that to work, Cherub would need an image of the seabed, one that's clear enough for her to lock down the endpoint for her portal."

"I'd send her one telepathically, while I was below the sea."

"That could work. Will you keep me informed on your progress?"

"That I shall. We'll keep the underwater pulley system going for now, and once we've reached the point where we need Cherub's aid, I'll reach out to her."

A squeal echoed up from the outer courtyard and Shaw crossed to her window and waved at Peigi flapping about in a large puddle. The girl was the youngest of their water fae, still a child of nine.

She blew a kiss to Peigi. "I have such fond memories of being her age, every new day being an adventure. This must all seem rather exciting to her, going through this Change and forging a tail."

"She's always wished for a tail, wished to be like the Sirens of the Sea."

"I did too at her age." Lilias released a long sigh. "To be young and carefree again."

"Aye, without a worry in the world." Shaw's smile was a reminiscing one.

"So, tell me your secret, Shaw." She gestured to the bailey. "'Tis raining outside, and with all that rain, how did you manage to cross the courtyard to reach this main tower of the palace?"

"I manipulated the rain to fall either side of me, then used some faerie dust to levitate when and where needed." He tapped his side where a leather pouch held his dust. "Keep your dust on you at all times. I've found it incredibly handy."

"I shall do so, and thank you for the tip." She scooted off the lid and crossed to her dressing table. After plucking the leather pouch of dust from her top drawer, she fastened the strap to her wrist, her dust and the pouch both spelled to repel water, so whenever she dived below the surface of the sea, it never got wet. Not that she could actually spell or make wishes below the sea. The dust always swirled away on the current and never landed where she needed it to land. "I will find the amulet, Shaw."

"I have no doubt you will." Shaw squeezed her shoulder and walked to the door. "Breena will be back amongst us in no time at all. I'll give your apologies to the others," he stated as he turned and left.

"Look after everyone for me," she called out, the velvet skirts of her turquoise gown sweeping to the floorboards, her bodice laced tight with crisscross straps at the back.

From her dresser, she picked up her brush and worked it through her locks, her hair more blond than her usual red this morn. That happened whenever she swam too much, the seawater leeching the red dye from her hair, and since she preferred looking at least a little different from her sisters, all three of them born identical in every way, she pinched some faerie dust from her pouch and sprinkled it over her hair with a quick wishing-spell. "With this dust, seal and conceal. Blond shall be gone, only red revealed."

Sparks flared from her fingertips, and she lowered her hand, her hair once more a vibrant red, the same shade as Breena's, a color she completely adored. Once more her friend returned to the forefront of her mind. "I'll find you soon, Breena. Ailith has told me that Levi and I will recover Ula's amulet, her senses strong with that knowledge. Once we have it, we'll use it to find and rescue you. Soon, Levi and I shall open a portal by way of a whirlpool and come to you. I have every faith we will."

"Princess, good morn." Esmae, the head maid for this wing of the palace, bustled into her chamber with her young daughter clutching her skirts. Esmae halted before her breakfast table and set the tray on top. "Cherub has arrived from the human realm and said she would join ye soon, so I've brought plenty for ye both."

"You have my thanks, Esmae." Smiling at wee Ailsa, she crouched as the girl seized her arm before releasing her mother's skirts, her feet bobbing an inch off the ground as she held tight to Lilias. The child possessed the skill of rising, an ability that caused her to remain insubstantial in weight, which meant unless she found a way to ground herself, usually by clutching onto someone, she could too easily float to the rafters as if she were no more than a feather sent aloft on a breeze. 'Twas a tricky skill to hold. "How are you this morn, Ailsa?"

"Mama said I can go and play with Peigi in the puddle soon. The water will drench my clothes and help hold me down." Glancing at her mother, Ailsa pleaded, "Can I go now, Mama?"

"Soon, my child." Esmae tickled Ailsa under her chin. "Drenched clothes or no', ye still cannae go outside without a leading strap on. Should the wind rise, ye'll be off and I'll spend the day chasing ye across the fields."

Ailsa giggled and turned her attention back to Lilias. "Is your tail the same pretty color as Peigi's?"

"Aye, 'tis the same. We all have pearl-colored scales."

"Ye willnae go missing like Breena, will ye?" The child pressed her small hand against Lilias's heart, her palm warm against the velvet of her bodice.

"I'm going to find Breena and bring her home. That I give you my word on." She covered Ailsa's hand with her hand and halted the child from floating higher. "My sister Ailith had a vision, and in it she saw a man named Levi, who's a fae-shifter from Murdock Matheson's clan, aiding me in finding the amulet. Once we have it, we'll be able to wish our way to Breena through a whirlpool."

"I've met yer Levi." Esmae bustled to the washstand and wiped up the water Lilias had spilled earlier.

"He's not *my* Levi. He's simply the warrior Cherub brought through from Matheson Castle to visit last week." She'd watched from her window as Levi had charmed her kin below in the bailey, the bairns fascinated as they circled him, the palace maids ogling him with far too much appreciation from the center well.

"I liked it when he shifted into his bear." Ailsa giggled.

"He shifted?" Well, she hadn't remained standing at her window long enough to see that. "I've never seen his bear. What's his animal like?"

"Very big. Very furry. He has very sharp teeth too."

"He let ye pet him, didnae he, my sweeting?" A glance at her daughter as Esmae tidied up the top of Lilias's dressing table. "He made ye so happy. He's a nice man, that Levi."

"Mama, he showed me how he apported things too. He made a coin appear out of thin air into his palm, and then he made it vanish behind my ear. All the other bairns clapped and cheered."

"He's very clever too." Esmae poured tea from the teapot on the table into two cups. "Can ye drink with no issue, Princess?"

"Aye, the merpeople can, so I should be able to with no issue." She held Ailsa's hand and transferred the child's grip to her mother's skirts, then eased into the chair before the table and stirred a spoonful of honey into her cup and brought the rim to her lips. Kicking her slippers off and tucking her feet to one side just in case her tail exploded from her, she tentatively sipped the drink. Letting out a relieved breath, she nodded at Esmae. "Thank heavens for that. I'm tired of flopping about on the floor."

"Aye, thank heavens, indeed." Esmae smiled at her daughter, tickled a finger under her chin. "I believe 'tis time for your paddle with Peigi in the puddle." They left with a wave.

Lilias took another sip of her tea.

"There you are." Cherub swished through her door, her flawless skin sparkling as bright and shiny as the stars which blazed within the portals she opened. Taking the chair beside hers, Cherub settled on the padded seat and squeezed her hand across the table. "Ailith told me about her vision. She said you and Levi will be the ones to find the amulet."

"Aye, 'tis true. Have you seen Levi this morn?" Cherub had returned to Matheson Castle with Cairstine.

"I have and he's worried about you, as is everyone at Matheson Castle. Murdock told me he'll be keeping a close eye on things too, which means we'll have two seers aiding us, him and Ailith." Cherub fluffed her blue velvet skirts, her bodice edged with white lace. "First though, we must speak more about you afore we leave."

"Speak away." She nudged Cherub's teacup toward her then chose a warm bread roll and smeared it with raspberry jam, while Cherub added orange marmalade to her roll and licked a drop of preserve from her fingertips.

"I brought with me a notebook." Cherub plucked a red leather notebook from her pocket and flipped it open.

"Since when did you start using a notebook?" She chewed on her roll.

"A few things have been slipping my mind these past few days. 'Tis unusual, I know."

"The fae have impeccable memories, never forgetting a thing."

"I'm hoping the issue will pass quickly." Cherub gave a rueful shake of her head as she read the first notation she'd written down. "First point I wished to ask. Do you have any feelings for Levi?"

"Pardon?" Shock widened her eyes. "No wonder you had to write it down. That isnae a question you'd usually ask."

"Well, obviously Ailith had a vision which included

the two of you together, and we both know you'll soon be mated to one of the unmated males at Matheson Castle, Levi being one of the remaining thirty-four. Secondly, you accepted a gift from him, a rather personal gift." Cherub gestured to the gold medallion at her neck. "That is a family heirloom."

"It wasnae a gift. 'Twas a prize from the wager he lost, and I do intend on returning it." She fingered the medallion, the chain nestling warmly against her skin, a keepsake his grandparents had given him, both grandparents she'd yet to meet.

"What wager?" Cherub arched a brow. "I didnae hear of any wager."

"He made a bet, said he could swim faster than me, which clearly isnae a possibility."

Levi had come stumbling out of the surf after their swim, his muscled chest bare and jeans drenched as he'd tossed the medallion to her, one he always wore. "*Well, I don't mind losing that bet since my medallion will look better on you than me anyway,*" he'd muttered. "*Even my grandparents would agree.*"

"*I would like to meet them, and why on earth did you think you'd win a swimming race against me?*" She'd slid the necklace over her head then wrung the hem of her blue undertunic.

"*They're with my parents enjoying a trip overseas, and I thought I'd win because I'm fast in the water. I always win the swimming races around here.*"

"*You might have in the past, but I'm not one of your clansmen.*" She'd smacked his arm, water spraying from her fingertips. "*You're also about as fast as a lump of lead.*"

Eyeing Cherub, the memory slowly fading away, she asked her aunt, "What was it like when you first met Kirk?"

"Oh, he was incorrigible."

"In what way?"

"I told him that the mated bond which had formed between us simply couldnae be. I was born to serve my people, had done so for over a thousand years, and that I didnae have time to accept the mated bond with him. Of course, he ignored my protestations, scooped me into his arms and walked off with me to a secluded bay."

"And then?" She leaned her chin on her upturned palms, her elbows pressed to the tabletop, her curiosity strong. She'd always enjoyed listening to Cherub's tales, and this one would be particularly interesting.

"Well, he showed me his bear then wheedled his way into my heart. Most frustrating, really." Cherub tore a bite from her roll. "I'll tell you exactly what happened once you're mated and no longer an innocent."

"I would rather know what to expect with my chosen one come the next full moon than be left with no notion at all."

"Hmm, well, the full moon isnae always the defining moment when the bond forges. Some mated pairs have known afore that moment arrived. Take Finlay Matheson for example." Cherub sipped her tea. "He knew Arabel was his mate the moment he met her, and there wasnae a full moon in sight. It all depends on who stirs you as no other can."

"Levi usually frustrates me. We have bickered many-a-time."

"Aye, but I've seen that he calms you as well." Cherub rose from the table and sashayed to the door, her long golden locks swaying down her back as she pocketed her notebook. "We dinnae have time to finish this conversation now, but we'll do so later. I have a few necessities to collect. Be ready to leave for Matheson Castle as soon as I return."

"I'll be waiting." She gnawed away on her roll, her thoughts crashing one over the other. Did Levi calm her as much as he frustrated her? Sometimes, aye.

Eyes closed, she sent her mind soaring out and reached the divide between their realms. A tiny gap quivered, and she flew through the break and blew out a grateful breath as she caught the glittering thread belonging to Levi. She followed his lifeforce and within mere moments sank deep into his mind. Looking out through his eyes, she caught water spraying from a nozzle above his head, the glass sides of a shower surrounding him, and steam pluming all around.

A shower. She'd always enjoyed bathing in one whenever she traveled to his twenty-first century time. Of course, she'd also admired the technology of his era, including the roads made of tar which allowed quick travel by whatever method of transport one chose. A miraculous invention. So too were the planes that flew from one country to another. Quite astonishing. 'Twas truly incredible to see how scientists and doctors had discovered cures and treatments to illnesses, how teachers performed an incredible feat in imparting and guiding the younger generations, and of how humanitarians cared for those who couldn't care for themselves. The human world seemed to be evolving at an ever-increasing pace. Humans had certainly embraced their shorter lifespans and not only survived but thrived.

Levi flicked the lever off and brought her thoughts tumbling back to him.

She waited quietly as he opened the shower door and crossed his bathroom floor of white marble glimmering with veins of silver-gray. He snagged a plush blue towel from a rail and turning, glanced at the mirror which hung above the vanity.

She snapped her eyes shut as he slung the towel around his hips, then peeked again as he secured it at his side.

Her mouth watered, his skin so slick and wet, his hair plastered to his head, water dripping from the dark ends and splattering his shoulders. He turned again, making her lose that delightful sight of him.

Flicking on a wall switch, he started a fan *whirring* overhead, the steam venting out. He had such a glorious bath that took up the entire wall on one side of the bathroom, was large enough to almost swim in, with water jets protruding from each side that would offer a wondrous massage. Jealousy roared through her. She would love such a bath here in the palace, but all she had was a metal tub she pulled before the fire.

Breathing deep, she shoved her jealousy aside and eyed Levi as he stood at the vanity and pressed his palms on the countertop. Intensely, he looked directly into his own fae-shifter eyes, the molten-gold depths swirling with such strong emotions. Need and worry among them.

Her body warmed and she pulled at her bodice and

tried to flap cooler air over her skin. He'd always had this impact on her, caused her heart to clench and heat to build in her middle, and why on earth was he still standing there in a towel with dewy drops all over his skin as he stared at himself?

Giving a shake of his head, he grabbed another towel and began scrubbing his hair dry, his gaze going down so that she couldn't help but catch each of the hard indents of his abdominal muscles bunching, his feet bare and perfect toes holding not a sliver of webbing as hers did. As he scrubbed, the movement of his hips had his hooked towel loosening. It slid lower, and she gulped. In a matter of seconds, it would slither down his legs and pool on the floor.

Shamelessly, she couldn't halt from ogling him. This might be one of those moments Cherub had spoken about. Did he stir her as no other could? Considering the heat building in her core and the tight pebbling of her nipples, the answer was aye. Did he calm her? Nay. She was anything but calm.

The towel managed to stay hooked in place as he finished drying his hair, and in the mirror, he angled his chin to one side and deepened his gaze. He seemed to look right at her. Aye, he'd locked gazes with her, as if he could sense her presence. Impossible, of course.

She'd gotten incredibly good at sneaking into people's minds through her telepathic skill and had no issue observing without their knowledge. If only she could sneak into Triton's mind, but his had always been out of reach of a telepath, the same as all of the merpeople were.

Levi leaned in closer to the mirror, his lips lifting in a

sudden, sultry quirk, one that made her heart begin to beat even harder and faster. Butterflies flapped about in her middle, their wings whooshing all about. A rumble suddenly filled his bathroom, vibrating in the very air.

Hello, Lilias, he mouthed silently in the mirror.

She clapped a hand over her mouth. He knew. Nay, he couldnae know she was in his mind. She'd done naught to give herself away. He must be testing her.

She remained quiet.

One second passed, two, then three.

He twitched one eyebrow up and chuckled, then did something for which she wasn't prepared.

He jerked the towel from his lean hips and dropped it.

Before she could slam her eyes shut, she caught the dark triangle of curls surrounding his manhood, his shaft thick and long as it swayed between his legs, and his balls…oh my. She'd seen his balls. Well, of course, that wasn't the first time she'd ever seen a man's balls, but it was the first time she'd seen Levi's. What a gorgeous specimen he was, all sleek and firm and rippling muscle.

I know you're there, he mouthed again in the mirror before he stalked into his bedchamber, leaving his bathroom door ajar. He proceeded to pull on a pair of black jeans, jiggled his front, and tucked himself away before zipping and fastening the dome. A belt came next, hooked into place, then he pulled a white shirt over his head that hugged every muscle in his upper body.

On a frustrating sigh, she flapped her bodice a bit more. He'd dressed far too quickly.

He returned to his bathroom, opened a drawer, and plugged his razor into the outlet, switched it on and ran the buzzing blades over his jaw. "Cat got your tongue?" he said out loud this time in the mirror.

She still wasn't going to answer him and give herself away.

"I can tell you're there," he uttered again, words that echoed within the four walls of his bathroom.

She huffed, not saying a word, because surely, he was still bluffing?

"I'm not sure how I can tell you're with me, but I can, Lilias."

She wasn't going to give in, wouldn't let him know he was right.

"Every time you've settled into my mind, I can sense your presence," he continued as he shaved.

"*Liar.*" She slammed a hand against her mouth. Ugh, how annoying. Why had she done that, spoken mind to mind with him? Now she'd gone and given herself away. "*You tricked me, Levi.*"

"*Hey, I heard you got a tail,*" he answered along the link, his shaver buzzing under his nose and down his neck.

"*Aye, which now goes rather well with my gills.*"

He frowned, turning his face this way and that in the mirror as he shaved spots he'd missed. "*I've never seen your gills. You always cover up in the water with a tunic. What do they look like?*"

"*They're no' very interesting, just thin feathery slits.*" She touched the organs along the sides of her middle that forced seawater out.

"*They sound amazing to me.*" He turned his razor off and stuck it back in his drawer before returning to his bedchamber. A soft whine came from a cane basket sitting on the floor near the head of his king-sized bed, a basket holding a bright burgundy and blue tartan blanket with two white paws reaching up to scratch the rim. A pink nose popped over the top, a wee puppy bouncing about to get a better look out. Big brown eyes pleaded for freedom, the puppy easily able to fit in her palms, the pup covered in thick white fur.

Her heart panged for Molly, the small dog she'd lost a year past when her pet had reached old age. Molly had been a wonderful companion, had adored running along the sandy shoreline of the beach and playing in the surf with her. When she swam, her pup had never ventured far from the shore, always waiting with absolute devotion for her return.

"Hey, meet my new dog, Minnie. Bella gave her to me. I would have just called her Pup, but Bella slapped me hard enough to almost cough out a lung. So, I went with Bella's choice of name, being Minnie. It's also an accurate description of the size of her. She's like a mini version of an actual dog."

"Bella's an empath, would never slap anyone."

"She's changed since getting mated to Jamie. Her momma-bear gene has kicked in now that she's pregnant."

"Oh my, she's with child? How exciting." She couldn't help but clap. *"There's to be another cub born at Matheson Castle. What wonderful news."*

"We're all celebrating the news, but now I've gotten a dog I didn't want." Levi scooped the pup up with one hand, eyed it nose to nose then deposited the wee thing in a litter box. Leaning one shoulder against the wall, he went quiet as he waited for Minnie to do her business.

"I'll take her. What breed is she?"

"She's a Maltese, and no, you can't take her. Bella would slap my other lung out if I gave Minnie away."

"Where did Bella get her?"

"She found the pup's mother seeking shelter in a cave deep in the woods. Abandoned, by the looks. The mother gave birth to three puppies. Bella gave the second one to Hunter and Ailith, and the third to Liam and Cairstine. The mother's name is Queen and Bella's keeping her."

"My sisters have no' said a word about getting new puppies." They never kept such things from each other.

"Maybe they were waiting for you to return to Matheson Castle before they introduced you to their new squirts."

"Aye, which is something they would do." She couldn't deny that.

"When you return, you can meet Minnie." He pushed off the wall and marched to his window, Minnie chasing after his heels and skidding all over the shiny floorboards, her paws going wide as she nosedived into a saucer filled with milk sitting only a few feet from Levi's feet.

Levi looked out over the inner courtyard below and she followed his sight to the men training in groups of two with bows and arrows. Arrow targets, about a hundred feet distant, were mounted on propped boards near the stony wall of the bailey. The men aimed and let their arrows soar and each arrow *thunked* into the bullseye with complete precision.

Levi bent and scratched behind Minnie's ear, and the puppy let out a contented noise that sounded just like a devoted sigh. Minnie blinked lazily at him then swiped her tongue over Levi's hand.

"*Your pup adores you.*" He was so good with animals. He'd easily soothed a skittish horse they'd found running loose when they'd gone riding within the forest the week afore. Then, when they'd returned to Matheson Castle, he'd noticed a dazed bird at the base of the curtain wall and picked it up. With great care, he'd tenderly checked the bird's wings then chosen a spot to release the bird at the edge of the meadow once it had revived itself. Together, they'd patiently waited a few steps away until the bird had launched skyward and disappeared over the treetops.

"*What's on your mind?*" he murmured between them.

"*Just lost in my thoughts.*"

"*Care to share them?*" Levi strode back and forth across the dark wood of his polished floorboards, the odd scratch here and there giving it a charming rustic appeal.

His chamber walls were painted blue and held a white trim with the odd splash of color about the room, as in the painting of a sunrise over the sea and a vase filled with bluebells that grew in abundance in the meadow. Along the entire length of the ceiling, aged wooden beams ran with recessed lighting positioned across them, and in one corner a comfortable blue velvet sofa beckoned, while the TV mounted to the wall was naught but a dark screen.

"*Would that be yay or nay?*" he asked, "*on sharing your thoughts?*"

"*I like your chamber. I also like watching the wildlife channel, particularly the programs that feature creatures of the sea.*"

"*Let me turn that channel on now.*" He opened his palm, the remote sitting on the table disappearing and reappearing again in his hand, an activation of his fae skill of apport. He could move objects from one place to another and make solid objects appear or materialize out of thin air, provided he knew the exact location of where those objects were. With the remote in hand, he hit the button and turned the TV on.

The screen flickered to life with images of the deep sea, and she released a soft sigh of longing, sounding far too much like Minnie had.

With a quick telling off, she cleared her throat and said, "*I miss the sea. I've been indoors for hours, would usually, by now, have gone out for a morning swim.*"

"*I miss the woods when I can't get outside, so I understand.*" He kept his gaze on the screen for her as he eased into a chair at his glass-topped corner table and pulled on a pair of worn leather boots.

Last week, Levi had invited her to enjoy a midday meal with him at that very table. He hadn't said why, but she'd soon found out since he'd all but quizzed her on her likes and dislikes. "*Why do you need to know all of this?*" she'd asked him at the time.

"*A man can get into trouble if he doesn't know the relevant details about his possible future mate,*" was what he'd answered.

"*Why do you think we might be mated?*" That's what she'd asked him, and he'd said that as one of the remaining thirty-four unmated males in his clan, he alone was the only one who felt so strongly about her.

Shaking her head, she forced herself to return to their current conversation. "*What's the weather like there? I wasnae paying enough attention when you were staring out the window at the archers.*"

"*The sky is clear, no rain in sight.*" He glanced out the window. White puffy clouds floated within a clear blue sky.

"You there, Levi?" A knock rattled his door. "It's Kirk."

"I'm coming." He crossed to the door and swung it open. "What's up?"

Kirk stood with his sword belted at his hip and thick leather guards encasing his forearms, a laptop propped under one arm. "We have a new case. There's a young lass by the name of Flora MacLeod downstairs. She's the librarian from Dunvegan Castle."

"I know Flora. We've chatted from time to time. Is she all right?"

"She's fine, but there's been a loss of an important heirloom at Dunvegan Castle. She brought a file with some pictures loaded on it of the item. I transferred a copy to this laptop. It makes for an interesting read. Look at the file, then meet me in the interview room."

"What makes it interesting?"

"She's lost a Celtic amulet, one that looks eerily similar to the description of Ula's amulet." Kirk handed the laptop across and left.

Levi closed the door and set the laptop on the table before powering the device up. "*This could be it, Lilias, the moment we find out more about the amulet.*"

"*Aye, can you show me the file?*"

"*I'm opening the file now.*" He tapped the screen just as Minnie scampered from her bowl to his feet and draped herself across the tips of his boots. Levi eyed the pup then with an agonized huff picked her up by the scruff of her neck and settled her in his lap.

"*I'll read it.*" Lilias ran her gaze down the lines of text and began,

"*Documented file compiled by Flora MacLeod of Dunvegan Castle.*

A valuable piece of heirloom jewelry belonging to Clan MacLeod of Dunvegan Castle, an amulet known as the Mother of Pearl, has been lost. The amulet is an ancient Celtic talisman that has been in the MacLeod's possession since the early twelve-hundreds, a gift bestowed to the young daughter of Balloch MacLeod, her name Sirena. The amulet was removed from a locked safe for the clan's celebration day, as is done each year, the amulet never shown to anyone from outside the clan.

During the celebration day, the entire clan enjoyed time together, picnicking and swimming and playing games along Loch Dunvegan. Over one-hundred members of the clan were present as the heirloom was passed around, so they might all have the opportunity to reflect upon their clan's history.

This heirloom, a Celtic circle with a large white pearl, was secretly bestowed upon Balloch's daughter by Ula, a Siren of the Sea, and 'tis said if wished upon, can transport the holder to whomever they desire. They need only speak their desired person's name."

Lilias's heart stopped. "*That's definitely Ula's amulet, the one that can take me to Breena,*" she whispered along their link, one hand clutched to her chest.

"Let's look at the pictures of it." He scrolled down the screen and inspected each attached image of the heirloom. *"What do you think?"*

"We've found it."

"Almost found it. It's lost, remember?" He lowered the laptop lid.

"Wait for me. I'll be there soon." She closed their link and dashed out the door to find Cherub. No more could they delay.

Chapter 4

Gently, Levi lifted Minnie from his lap and settled her on the plush blue covers of his bed. From a shelf in his wardrobe, he collected his sword belt and strapped it on, slid his sword into the holster and selected his two favorite daggers, sheathed one at his left wrist and tucked the other into his right boot. His cell phone chirped from his bedside table, and he picked it up on the third ring, the display showing the call coming from Liam.

"What can I do for you?" he asked as he scooped up Minnie and tucked her against his chest.

"I heard Flora MacLeod from Dunvegan Castle is here. Word is her clan has lost an amulet."

"News travels fast, and aye, they have." He left his chamber, jogged down the hallway and took the stairs two at a time to the ground floor.

"Is it *the* amulet?" his cousin queried.

"Aye."

"Have you spoken to Lilias, caught her up?"

"Aye."

"You sound out of sorts. Is everything all right?"

"I miss her when she's not here." He snapped those words out with each step he took.

"You have to take care, Levi. There are thirty-four unmated males in this clan, and you might not be her chosen one. Try to set your feelings for her aside until the full moon. You've only got a few days to wait."

"That's not how you handled it with Cairstine." His bear rumbled deep inside him.

"Cairstine is in a league of her own."

"I know, I know, she's a scary-ass dragon who breathes fire and likes burning everything down." Their whole clan had been aware that if Liam hadn't completed the bond with Cairstine when he had, that his mate would have Turned into one of the Bloodthirsty and caused chaos to reign as her fire scorched the Earth and she killed without care. He crossed the ground floor foyer and pushed through the double doors into the great hall. "Hey, can we talk later? I've got a puppy sitter to find and then a meeting to join."

"Of course. Reach out to me if you need someone to talk to. I'm always here."

"Thanks, Liam." He hung up, pocketed his cell, and strode around the perimeter toward the servery where breakfast had been laid out. Alina stood at the heated pan turning the bacon and sausages, the thirteen-year-old loading up a plate for one of his clansmen.

Sidling up to Alina, who adored animals, he knocked shoulders with her. "You feel like a companion for the day?"

"Oh, aye, as long as you mean Minnie." Grinning, she handed him her cooking tongs, nabbed Minnie from him and stuck the puppy down the front of her zippered sweatshirt, the pup pawing back up until her tiny head poked out from the top. After breaking off a piece of bacon from a strip, Alina blew on it until it cooled then fed it to Minnie with a soft murmur and a rub of her cheek against the pup's cheek. "Little one, we've got to get you to grow, otherwise you'll be the runt of your mother's litter forever. We can't let that happen." Alina ducked a look at him, a hopeful look. "I wish I could keep her."

"You can be her second parent, right after me." He held up one hand for a high five. "What do you say?"

"Aye, I say aye." She slapped her hand against his.

"Can you keep her safe until I return for her? I've got a meeting, then a hunt to find a lost amulet."

"I'll keep her for as long as you need, and everyone's talking about Lilias getting a tail." She pointed to the bacon. "Hey, I gave you the tongs for a reason. You're supposed to be turning the meat or it'll burn."

"Aye, aye, little one." Chuckling, he flipped the bacon and rolled the sizzling sausages about. "Have you seen our chief this morning?"

"Murdock's already been down, grabbed a bite and headed out. He took his horse to the headland. Said he needed a ride and some fresh air to see if another vision would arise. He's really worried about Lilias, hopes he can get a tag on Breena's location."

"We'll take the aid of any seer who offers it and speaking of aid," he stated as he handed the tongs back to her, popped a kiss on the top of Alina's head. "I'd better get moving to this meeting and aid Kirk, otherwise he'll bring out those bagpipes of his and torture us all again by trying to play them."

"He wants to learn a new skill now that he's an immortal and has time." She added tomato slices to the grill, the juices sizzling and sending a tantalizing buttery tomato scent into the air. "What would you do if you lived forever?"

"Learn all of the martial arts. You?"

"Learn as many languages as I could."

"Perhaps you could suggest that to Kirk. I'd rather hear him fumble his way through the languages than those bagpipes." With a wink, he pinched a bacon slice and headed out of the great hall and along the labyrinth of passageways toward the interview room.

At the door, he knocked and walked into the room painted a stark white with only a square metal table and metal-backed chairs as furniture. A two-way mirrored glass pane was affixed on one wall, while in the upper corner near the ceiling, the red camera light glowed as the device logged the conversation currently underway between Kirk and Flora. Standard procedure, just in case one of them needed to play it back, look for any missed information.

"Good morning, Flora." He strode across and shook the petite blonde's hand, the tinted glasses she always wore hiding her eyes, her red woolen cardigan buttoned over white jeans. "Great to see you, although I'm sorry to hear about the loss of your amulet. Do you need me to dim the lights?"

"Aye, please. I see you've remembered my sensitivity to light?"

"It's hard to forget when I don't know anyone else with the issue. You're rather unique." He dimmed the lights, and she nodded her head in thanks as he sank into the chair across from her. "What causes it, if you don't mind me asking?"

"My irises are very pale. They simply don't have enough pigmentation to protect them against bright light." She tapped her darkened glasses higher on her nose. "I wished to ask. Did you find your favorite set of daggers you left at the blacksmith's shop?"

He snorted a laugh. He'd bumped into Flora at the blacksmith's shop last week. She'd been picking up a blade while he'd been waiting for the blacksmith's son to find his daggers. "Aye, but I had to sail across the loch to Eileen Donan Castle and collect them from their castle armorer. The blacksmith's son gave them to the wrong customer. How's the transcribing going at your keep? You said you're working your way through some extremely old scrolls."

"It's slow going since some of the text dates back several centuries. Most of the scrolls seem to be a mix of the old Celtic languages, mostly Gaelic, but some Irish, Manx, Breton, Cornish, and Welsh thrown in. I'm fluent in all of them, but the ink isn't as legible on the scrolls in some places as it is in others. I'm having to take a stab at some of the missing text."

"You seem too young to have mastered all of the old languages. You couldn't be more than twenty-two or twenty-three."

"Twenty-five, and I've grown up at the knee of our MacLeod clan elders. They teach the languages to the bairns from the moment we can speak. Celtic languages actually become second nature for us to read and converse in, except it'll take a few years to transcribe all the scrolls into electronic format, although I'm in it for the long haul, as they say." She quirked a brow. "I also heard clan Matheson are hosting the next Highland Games. What events will you be competing in?"

"The Caber Toss." He hiked his thumb toward Kirk. "Kirk has offered to play the bagpipes, and I suggest you steer clear of him when he brings them out. In fact, I'll pay you to tutor him on the old languages. He needs a better hobby."

"I'm getting better at the pipes every day." Kirk settled back in his chair, a grin tugging at his lips. "My wife says I might only scare away half the crowd at the Games, so I'm taking that as a win."

"You're wed?" Flora asked Kirk as she straightened in her chair. "I hadn't heard. Might I have met her?"

"She's new to the area. Her name is Cherub."

"What an unusual name, although I've heard of it once before. Now where did I…" She tapped the tabletop, hummed under her breath. "Oh, I remember now, it was in one of the scrolls I transcribed recently. There was a tale about a faerie princess named Cherub. The tale was incredibly divine. Your wife has a mythically renowned name."

"Her parents actually named her after *that* Cherub, and speaking of her, Cherub and another of our clanswomen will be here very soon, asked that we wait until their arrival before we discussed your case." Kirk eased back in his chair, crossed his feet at his ankles. "While we wait, tell us what your favorite event is?"

"For the Games?"

"Aye."

"Well, I'm rather respectable at Shifting the Stones." She pushed her cardigan sleeves up and flexed her biceps. "I might be short, but I have surprisingly strong arms. It comes from heaving all those dusty tomes around all day."

"I believe you."

"So do I." Levi chuckled. "What about your father? Calder's impossible to beat with the Stones. He lifts them from the ground and drops them onto the barrels as if he could do it all day. I get tired about just thinking of competing against him in that event."

"My father actually rebuilt the crumbling stone walls surrounding the water gardens at Dunvegan Castle. It's been exceedingly good practice for the Stones event."

"That explains a lot." The water gardens at Dunvegan Castle were stunning and incredibly special, a place Levi had always enjoyed when visiting Dunvegan Castle.

"*Cherub and I are here*," Lilias whispered breathily in his mind. "*Behind the two-way mirrored glass.*"

Levi's heart skipped a beat, the return of her presence in his mind causing a slow burn to warm his middle and catch the attention of his bear.

"*We're coming in now.*" She opened the door and continued to hold it open for Cherub who slipped inside. As Lilias shut the door, her turquoise gown swayed about her slippered toes, her bodice laced tight with crisscross straps at the back, and the bare skin of her neck, on delicious display, making his mouth water.

He wanted to continue soaking in the returned sight of

her, except Cherub stepped in between them and eyed him with an arch of one regal brow from under the hood of her white fur cape. As the eldest of the faerie king's children, Cherub had been born with the defining mark of the firstborn, sparkling skin, which she always hid when meeting people from outside of clan Matheson. She would keep her skin hidden this morning from Flora too. He had no doubt she would.

"Levi," Cherub whispered as she bent to his ear, "cease staring at my niece as if you want to eat her. Perform the introductions, if you will."

"My apologies." He eyed Flora and gestured to Cherub. "Flora, meet Cherub, Kirk's wife, and Lilias, both valuable members of our team. They'll be aiding Kirk and me in the search for your lost heirloom."

"It's a pleasure to meet you both." Flora shook hands with Lilias, who sat beside him, then nodded at Cherub as she sat next to Kirk. "Kirk said you'd recently wed. Congratulations on your nuptials."

"You have my thanks." Gently, Cherub cupped Kirk's cheek, her fingers gloved in white satin, and Kirk caught her hand and brought her knuckles to his lips for a kiss.

Lilias smiled at Flora, the medallion she'd won from him glinting at her neck, the piece certainly stunning where it lay nestled against her creamy skin.

He gave his head a shake, brought himself back from his musings.

"I've seen pictures of your amulet. 'Tis beautiful," Lilias said to Flora. "Can you provide more information?"

"Well, I'll try, but no one can remember who was the last to hold it during our celebration day, but I believe it must have been one of the bairns. The wee ones were so busy playing tag that day down by the shore. Some of them were running in and out of the water, others splashing about near the rocks, while some of the older bairns swam out quite deep and surfed in with the waves." Flora glanced at Levi. "I realize your clan usually works government cases, but this amulet is worth more than I can express with words. We even keep it locked away in a safe, other than for our celebration day. My clan and I have searched the area where we held our festivities, both on land and in the water, but now we fear if the amulet isn't found soon that it will be lost to us forever. I know your clan holds great expertise in investigation and tracking, thought you might be able to offer some insight from an outsiders' point of view? Perhaps, even, if you might, could you speak to each of the young ones. You might be able to gather more information than I have."

"Sometimes all it takes is the right question to bring forth the right answer." Levi would leave no stone unturned in tracking down the amulet.

Kirk cleared his throat, queried, "Can you guide us through the full chain of events, Flora? You said you keep the amulet locked in a safe. Perhaps begin from the time you took it out."

"Of course." Flora nodded profusely. "I took it out the night before the celebration day. We keep the amulet locked away in my father's solar. I'd just keyed in the numbers of the safe and retrieved it when I heard a terrible crash outside. I looked out the window and saw one of the walkway statues toppled on the ground, the head broken into shards along the cobbles. A man stood over it, a man I thought for a moment was our chief, his visage similar, but of course it wasn't."

"Who was it?" Kirk asked.

"Not our chief. He usually resides at Dunvegan with his family, except at present he's attending to business matters in the city, is still there unfortunately, and couldn't even attend our celebration day." She leaned forward. "The hour was late, nearly midnight, and even though I had the amulet in my hand, I hurried outside and that's when the man took off toward the stairs leading down to the loch. I chased after him to the sea-gate and when I reached the landing, whoever it was dove into the water. They surfaced about twenty feet out from shore. They had a large silhouette from what I could make out, and I swear, well, I saw something strange, hind flippers of some sort when they dove again, a seal's flippers. When he surfaced, his head resembled a seal's as well, and there wasn't just one of them. Another seal appeared out beside the first, a second creature." She chewed her lower lip. "I realize that sounds strange, but our Celtic heritage is rich with varied beliefs, traditions and customs, which is why I'm certain I saw a man turn into a selkie seal." Her glasses slid forward on her nose, and she pushed them back before casting a sharp turn of her head at each of them. "They saw the amulet. I was shouting at them and shaking my hand with it fisted between my fingers."

"You've mentioned them for a reason. If you did see two selkie seals, do you believe they might have come back for it during your celebration day?" Levi asked her.

"I haven't told you everything, but there is a legend surrounding Ula's amulet. It's said that a selkie seer first told Ula to hide the amulet on Earth, far away from her greatest enemy, a man named Triton, the son of Poseidon. That's why Ula gave the amulet to Balloch MacLeod's daughter in the twelve-hundreds. The girl's name was Sirena, and it's said she had close ties with Ula through Balloch." Flora tapped her steepled fingers together. "I am a librarian, tasked with keeping the history of my clan intact. I've read many accounts written in the hands of my own clan, of stories told through the centuries about the other realms. I'm wondering if the selkies who visited that night returned the next morning and found a way to walk among my clansmen before stealing the amulet away."

"So, perhaps not lost by one of the bairns?" Levi poured everyone a glass of water from the water jug in the center of the table and sipped his own.

"Maybe, maybe not." Frowning, Flora's eyebrows pinched together. "There is seer blood that runs through my father's maternal line, blood that sometimes speaks to me, and I had the distinct sense I had to come to clan Matheson for aid, not just because of your fine investigative skills, but because your clan has seer blood running through it too. My father and I both know Murdock Matheson is a seer. We've spoken to him a time or two about his visions, and my own of course since I get them on occasion. Not that my ability is as strong as his. It's nowhere near his level."

"Well, thank you for your honesty." He reached across and squeezed her hand resting on the table before settling back in his chair again. "We will keep all you've said in mind, but obviously Dunvegan Castle is also a tourist hot spot on the Isle of Skye, which means we also need to cover other bases. Could you provide a list of the names of everyone, including your clansmen and the tourists who came onto MacLeod property during your celebration day? We must have the full list."

"There were only a few visitors during the day, but I thought you might ask for such a list, so I brought one with me." She scooped her canvas satchel from the floor beside her chair and set a piece of paper on the table, names scrawled on both front and back. "On the front side are my clansmen's names and their bairns. On the back are the names of two local families who arrived, both wishing to enjoy the gardens that day since the weather was so lovely. They hold lifetime passes, and apart from those people, we had the doors to Dunvegan closed to all other visitors."

"I'll take a copy of the list, if you don't mind." Levi pulled his cell phone from his pocket and *clicked* a picture before passing the list to Kirk.

"How do you wish to proceed from here?" Flora asked as she set her satchel back on the floor.

"We'll use all our investigative skills," Kirk stated as he eyed the paper positioned so both he and Cherub could read it. "And take into account all you've spoken about, including the selkies and the other realms. We'll be at Dunvegan Castle no later than this evening. Do you have rooms we could use for the duration of our stay? It might take a few days to speak to everyone on your list."

"I'll make sure rooms are prepared."

"Excellent, then we'll talk more this evening. I'll see you to your car." Kirk pushed his chair back, rounded the table to Flora and guided her out the door. They disappeared down the hallway, their voices drifting away as they chatted.

"She believes in the realms. I adore her already." Cherub pushed her hood back as she eyed Lilias. "We'll make firm friends, I'm sure."

"I agree." Lilias smiled at Cherub. "Do you intend on showing her your sparkly skin when we arrive? Or mayhap I should show her how I can clothe myself with one wave of my hand, and forge a tail." She swept a hand down her body, her gown shimmering away and jeans and a loose sweater appearing in its place.

"Oh my, I've always been envious of your ability to fashion clothes from the air." Cherub caught Lilias's hands. "No more being cheeky about exposing exactly who we are. I'll join Kirk outside and we shall meet you and Levi in the bailey in an hour. Does that sound suitable?"

"Of course." Lilias glanced at Levi. "Does that sound suitable to you too?"

"Absolutely."

"Wonderful," Cherub murmured as she walked to the door. "And, Lilias, dinnae forget about our conversation earlier this morn." Cherub closed the door behind her.

"What conversation would that be?" Levi seized Lilias's hips and, with a squeal from her, yanked her into his lap. He was done with keeping his distance from her, and they were all alone for the first time in days. He intended on taking every advantage of it. "I've missed you."

"What are you doing?" She grasped his arms, her legs tipping up.

"Tell me about the conversation."

"Well, Cherub said she'd learned that the full moon isnae always the defining moment when the bond forges.

Some mated pairs have known afore that moment arrived. She gave Finlay Matheson as an example. He knew Arabel was his mate the moment he met her, and there wasnae a full moon in sight. It all depends on who stirs me, or so Cherub says." She swept her hand down his body and his shirt shimmered away.

"Hey, where did it go?" He searched the room for his shirt.

"I dropped it in the loo." Her lips twitched up.

"Liar. Shirt," he muttered as he snapped his fingers. "And leave my jeans on. I've already been naked in front of you today."

"Are you talking about your shower?" She fluttered a hand over his chest and returned his shirt, the fabric settling over his skin.

He caught her fingers before she could pull them away, turned her hand over within his own and rubbed his thumbs along the center of her palms. Her emerald eyes darkened, and longing surged inside him, just as it always did when he got this close to her, got to look so deep into her beautiful eyes with those glorious flecks of gold.

Desire beat fiercely within his chest and pounded outward. He'd never experienced these kinds of emotions with anyone else. Only ever with her. He'd missed her terribly, and now, it felt so right holding her hand, to have her this close again. For five long years, he'd been searching for his chosen one, had awaited the night of the full moon each month that had passed, and when he'd begun the chase, it had led him directly to the water's edge of one loch or another within the Highlands. On those nights, he'd stripped off and dived into the water, then swum in endless circles, going nowhere, and finding no one. "I struggle to keep my hands off you," he admitted to her.

"You are rather handsy. Cherub tells me Kirk suffers the same dilemma."

"That's because they're mated." He traced over her wrist, up her arm and over her shoulder toward her neck. With her red locks sliding sensuously against the back of his hand, he cradled her nape, the color of her hair more vibrant than it had been a few days past. He cleared his throat, returned his gaze to her. "Lilias, have you ever had feelings for another?"

"I adore my sisters."

"I meant a man."

"I adore my father."

He wanted to smack her backside. "Other than a male family member," he muttered.

"I've been waiting over eight-hundred years to find my chosen one and my sisters and I had almost lost all hope until Ailith discovered her mated bond taking form with Hunter. Now Cairstine has Liam, and I'm rather jealous of them both."

"That doesn't answer my question." Her sweater held a deep V neck, no blouse or shirt donned underneath, the soft white wool molding itself to her womanly curves. He rocked back on the legs of his chair, his sweet water nymph leaning in closer, her head tipped to one side as she gave him a curious look. He lowered his gaze and got rewarded with a tantalizing view of the creamy upper swells of her breasts. Deep in his middle, his animal rumbled and urged him to take a lick of what she offered.

No holding back.

Their conversation was done, and he much preferred action over words.

Always had, always would.

He dipped his head and licked across the seam of her lips. As she arched her neck and showed him the beating pulse point in her neck, a scorching heat sizzled down his spine and caught fire in his groin. He wanted to mark her, wanted her to mark him in return, and it couldn't wait.

Both he and his bear wanted more.

"Levi." She slapped a hand over his mouth, halting him from making the move he desperately wished to make. Glancing at the camera mounted on the wall, she murmured, "Mayhap we should take this conversation to a place where we arenae being taped. Your bedchamber?"

"I couldn't agree more." With a low growl, he hoisted to his feet and slung her over his shoulder. His woman had made a request, and he intended on honoring it. Aye, his woman. He was certain she was his and he was about to take her to his chamber where he'd have her all to himself. The day was finally getting better.

Chapter 5

Having returned from a brisk ride, Murdock Matheson stood at his solar window on the second floor of Matheson Castle and rested his hands on the windowsill as the wind blew in across the loch, the seagulls overhead screeching. Below in the inner courtyard, the heavy wooden front door of their keep swung open. Murdock leaned out farther, caught Kirk leading Flora MacLeod across the inner courtyard and through the main gate under the portcullis. The librarian started her red sedan and waved out the open window to Kirk before driving away down the private gravel road, which wound for several miles through the forest before it reached the main highway.

A vision suddenly swirled before his eyes, and he grasped ahold of the images.

Finally, this was what he'd been waiting for, what he'd been trying to push to the surface since his vision last evening of Lilias at Loch Heart. He urged the images to take a firm, solid form and they slowly did, crystalizing fully in his mind.

A water garden.

It slowly shimmered into full view.

He'd seen that water garden many-a-time. It graced the formal gardens of Dunvegan Castle, where Flora, who'd just left, resided. The gardens were a stark contrast to the barren moors and craggy mountains that dominated the Isle of Skye's landscape. The formal gardens, including the water garden, were fed by shimmering waterfalls and large streams that flowed down from the mountains out to the sea.

The water garden held ornate bridges that spanned small garden islands awash with a rich and colorful variety of plants, a stone wall built around the full exterior of the gardens, a wall rebuilt and maintained by Flora's father, Calder MacLeod, a man Murdock had known his entire life. A man who held secrets about his lineage just as clan Matheson did, secrets Murdock had uncovered as a seer many years ago, secrets he couldn't speak of unless Calder and Flora chose to speak of them first.

Murdock narrowed his vision and searched within the gardens.

A watery image of Lilias slowly fluttered to full vision, and he kept his second sight on her as she sat down on an elegant iron bench next to a trickling stream flowing into a garden pond. A man strode toward her in the dark of the night. It was Levi, one of the thirty-four remaining unmated shifter males within his keep, although going by the covetous look in Levi's eyes as he walked with purpose toward Lilias, things were clearly about to change.

Lilias wore a gauzy white silken gown that swept just

past her knees, her long red locks swaying down her back, her bare feet digging into the lush grass as she stood to meet Levi as he joined her, the scales on Lilias's calves glinting in the moonlight. Saying not a word, Levi looked deep into her eyes, and a long minute seemed to pass before Levi finally spoke.

"How'd your search of the seabed go?" he asked her.

"'Twas a bust as you and those in your era would say." She wriggled her toes again, and Levi lowered to a crouch and eyed the webbing between her toes, his gaze going up to her ankles and then to her calves.

"May I touch your scales?" he asked, and she gave a silent nod.

Gently, Levi ran one finger along the line of shimmery pearl-colored scales covering her calves. She wobbled but managed to grasp his shoulders to hold herself steady.

Levi rose, leaned in and whispered in her ear, "The full moon is tomorrow eve, but I'm not sure I'll make it. I want to ravish you tonight."

From the position of their bodies and Levi's words, these two appeared mated, and currently in need of their privacy.

Lately, Murdock had been receiving more visions of late of mated bonds taking form, which was promising but also signified that danger currently loomed for his kin. These visions were a warning he couldn't ignore, because deep in his soul, he sensed greater turmoil coming for Lilias and Levi. The water fae were becoming pawns in Triton's game to outwit Poseidon.

He opened his eyes and allowed his vision to melt away.

It was just as well that the selkie seer, Aisling, had told Lilias that Ailith was the one she needed to speak to about any possible visions, because right now Murdock's hands were tied. He couldn't abuse the trust Flora and Calder had placed in him all those years ago, which meant he couldn't warn his kin of what awaited them at Dunvegan Castle. Couldn't warn them at all. They'd be going in blind.

Chapter 6

"All I can say is, I mean, well, obviously the mated bond is a very sacred union and none of the fae are permitted to breach its creation or completion. Which is why we must be absolutely certain we're mated afore we kiss again." Flustered, Lilias perched on the end of Levi's bed, her hands sinking into his plush blue bedcovers, the color reminding her of the hue of the sea under the vivid warmth of the sun. She kept her gaze down, tried not to allow it to rise and take in the wondrous sight of Levi standing over her. She only had to be in the same room as him for her emotions to escalate.

"Lilias?" Levi murmured her name in a husky voice. "Ever since your arrival, I've both hoped for and feared the coming full moon. Hoped I'd sense the deep need to begin my chase of you and feared it would be another one of my clansmen who did." He leaned over her farther, touched his nose to her neck and breathed deep, in the way a bear did when savoring the scent of its next meal.

"Tell your bear to settle, Levi Matheson." She leaned back to gain an inch or two and the mattress rippled beneath her, as if water were contained within. She pushed both palms down hard and the mattress rolled. Aye, his mattress most definitely contained water. Wide-eyed, she looked at him. "What is this sorcery?"

"It's a waterbed." A devilish glint lit his eyes.

"I've never heard of such a thing."

"Let me show you how it works." Crawling in over top of her, he made the water move underneath them both.

"Where on earth did you find it?" She jiggled about and waves rolled.

"Curious, hmm?"

"Aye, please tell me." She jerked one corner of the bedcovers aside and exposed the mattress. It had a thick blue bladder tucked within. "'Tis incredible."

"I bought it online, had it delivered a few days ago." A satisfied smile, like the one he'd had when they'd been out in the forest recently together.

They'd been taking a walk when she'd stumbled upon a picnic lunch spread out on a dark green and white tartan blanket. Gasping, she'd almost crushed a loaf of deliciously warm homemade bread. Levi had caught her around the waist and pulled her back, then proceeded to offer her a place on the blanket next to a basket overflowing with shiny red apples, plump apricots, and a glorious bunch of purple grapes. He'd admitted he'd wanted to surprise her with the picnic, and she'd certainly been surprised. Once she'd sat, he'd made them both honey sandwiches and then proceeded to devour his, honey the food she'd soon learned his bear absolutely adored. Gently, she'd wiped away a smear of honey which had coated his chin, her giggles echoing through the trees. The moment had been incredibly surreal.

Shaking her head, she returned to the moment and frowned at him. "What secrets are you hiding? You've acquired a new puppy and now a new waterbed."

"I'd like to acquire you too." He brushed the backs of his fingers down her neck and back up again, then stroked his thumb fleetingly over her lower lip. Delicious tingles radiated out from that sensitive spot and caused heat to gather in her middle. "You clearly like my bed," he whispered with a lick of her ear. "The bladder has a hydro support system, and the water can be warmed to whatever temperature is desired, which helps to ease any sore muscles while one sleeps."

"I'm about to melt into this mattress." And melt into his sensual voice.

"There is a bond growing between us." He brushed a finger over her lower lip. "One that increases in strength each day we're together, and full moon or not, it's time for us to allow that bond to take a deeper hold. I want to kiss you, Lilias, again and again." He leaned closer, his lips a mere breath away from hers. "I also want you to kiss me back."

She couldn't ignore the truth before her, of how her heart lurched toward him at his nearness, of how she wanted to wrap her arms around his neck and draw him even closer. No one could halt a mated bond from forming. No one could halt those ties from strengthening should they be a *true* pair of the heart and soul.

She licked his lower lip, but needed so much more, so

she took.

She kissed him, their mouths joining together and his breath flowing so sweetly over her tongue. Oh, he was all hard muscle. Arms wrapped around his neck, she delved deeper into his mouth and kissed him the same way as he kissed her, with all the fierce need they held for each other roaring to full and vibrant life.

"You're making me feel hot." Heat pounded through her blood.

"Likewise." He clamped her backside tight and kissed her again, his hips rocking against her hips and his hard shaft poking into her belly.

She'd never joined with another man, not when she'd been diligently awaiting her mate's claiming, but that didn't mean she wasn't aware of the intimacies that occurred between a man and a woman, not when one had lived as long as she had.

Far too often, and in all manner of places, she'd stumbled upon heated exchanges between her fae kind. From within the woods nestled close to her grandfather's stronghold to within the sea between mated water fae. Whenever she'd come across a couple, she'd always tried to discreetly back away and leave the pair alone. Usually, she was successful, disappearing without anyone the wiser, but there had also been times when she'd been secretly captivated by the act of pure love on display, had been unable to turn away and leave. Sometimes, she'd remained hidden and watched as the fierce intensity of the mated bond bloomed to full and vibrant life. 'Twas not always in the physical joining itself, but in the devotion and passion that blazed in a mated pair's eyes for each other. That kind of love transcended time itself.

Levi caught her hand and pressed it against his thumping heartbeat, his body molded to her body until he'd left not one inch of them separated, the mattress underneath rolling gently as they floated atop it, his gaze locked on her.

"I need to say something," he whispered between them. "I've seen the bond being forged between a mated pair. I even asked Hunter and Liam what it felt like for them. They spoke of the all-consuming need they had for their chosen ones, and I feel that same need for you. It's intense, but I need to hear you say you feel the same way about me."

Aye, Ailith had been unable to deny the bond with Hunter, or Cairstine with Liam, and the same fierce emotions her sisters had spoken of were currently raging through her.

"Lilias?" He searched her gaze. "Answer me, please."

"I think about you constantly." She bit her inner lip.

"Do you think you could elaborate on that?"

"Only if you show me the full wave effect of this mattress." Another bite.

"Is that your way of saying your need is intense?" He had such sinfully suggestive eyes.

"Mates cannae lie to each other. You'd be able to sense it if I did."

"Then, when my lady asks, I provide." Rubbing his body against hers, he began rocking them. Slowly at first, then as he dipped his head and nuzzled her neck, he increased his speed.

She slipped one hand underneath the hem of his white shirt that clung tightly to every muscle in his upper body.

Palming his heated flesh, she let out a dreamy sigh. "I am drawn to you, Levi, cannae help but seek you out telepathically when there is any form of distance between us, and I sense, to the depths of my soul, that I am also Changing into one of the merpeople and there is naught I can do about it."

"You're not going to Change. We're going to find the amulet, then find and free Breena from Triton's hold. We'll reverse whatever spell he's spoken to create your tails." He growled the words, his bear emitting a loud rumble, fur suddenly sprouting underneath her hand against his skin, the soft pelt there one moment then gone the next.

"Your bear is incredibly close to the surface. I have yet to even meet him. What's he like?" A sudden and fierce need to know his other half roared through her. "You showed wee Ailsa."

"That's because she asked." He covered her hand with his, his fingers trapping hers against his skin. "I'll bring him out, but be forewarned, he'll likely act territorial around you."

"As long as he keeps his sharp claws off this mattress and does no' burst the bladder, then we will get along just fine."

"No springing a leak. Got it." He pushed upright, left her on the bed and stood in the center of his chamber. Fur rippled across his arms as he gripped his shirt hem and hauled it over his head. Shirt tossed aside, he unzipped his jeans then halted as he met her gaze, his lips slowly lifting. "This moment is eerily similar to this morning, don't you think?"

"Aye, but in reverse. You're stripping instead of

dressing. Allow me to give you some privacy." Grinning, she scooted off the bed and gave him her back. "Is that better?"

"I've never needed privacy from you." He kicked off his boots with a *thump*, then the whisper of denim and the clank of metal teased her senses as he removed his weapons and clothing. "Turn around. I like having your eyes on me, my sweet water nymph."

"In all honesty, I'm quite partial to having them on you too." Since she had no desire to keep staring at his wall, she turned and caught her breath as Levi stood before her completely naked, his clothing a puddle at his feet.

Levi winked and sparks flared, a lightning bright display that had Lilias blinking against the vivid glare. As the glow dispersed, one very large bear with silky dark fur reared up onto his hind legs and roared. The beast dropped back down, his paws slapping hard against the floor, his teeth sharp and very lethal looking.

"Oh my." Lilias jerked back, coming up hard against the wall, her heartbeat racing. Levi stalked toward her with a hungry snarl. His bear was here, and she was about to meet him. "I hope I'm not your next meal. The water fae are half fish. Bears like eating fish, aye, but no' this fish?"

He heaved up again, his paws coming down hard on the wall either side of her head, then he went completely still and whined as if he'd not meant to scare her. His tongue lolled out and swept across her cheek, then he made another soft whimpering sound that melted her, but also brought out her teasing side.

"I'll end up flopping about on the floor with a tail if you keep slobbering all over me." Wiping her face, she was rather grateful to still be standing on both feet.

Gently, she laid her hands on his head, patted between his silky ears, his fur soft and luxurious underneath her palms. His pelt tickled her fingertips.

Slowly, she caressed down his neck and rubbed under his chin, his deep, hungry purr causing an intense need to surge through her. Meeting his bear filled her entire being with satisfaction. He'd shared a part of himself, a deeply intimate part. "You have a pretty bear, Levi."

He growled, his eyes narrowing.

"Oh, did I say pretty? My apologies. I meant reasonably pretty."

Another growl.

"All right, he's handsome, in a very gruff and manly way. That better?"

His growl tapered away, and he stuck his nose into her neck. One long sniff, his bear getting growly again, this time not in anger but clear hunger.

"Dinnae lick me again," she warned in her most threatening tone.

He dropped to his paws and rubbed his side against her legs.

Crouching, she sank her hands deeper into his silky pelt, stroked down his back and over his rump. Touching him so freely made her heart swell with more need. He'd given her a gift by sharing all of himself with her this day.

Lights shimmered and blazed all about him, and she toppled back onto the floor.

Levi sprang over top of her, naked, hard, and hot. "My bear wants you. I want you, and nothing and no one will keep us apart another day longer. You are my mate, Lilias, and I'll do whatever it takes to keep you safe."

"As I will to keep you safe too." She rubbed his wide chest, the smattering of dark hair thinning as it flowed between his rigid abdominal muscles and trailed down to his nether region. Swallowing hard, she couldn't keep her hand or her gaze from moving down to that part of him. She touched the dark curls surrounding his manhood which rose thick between his legs. His shaft got even longer. She licked her dry lips.

"I'm yours," he whispered with a guttural tone. "My body, my heart, and my soul, Lilias."

"There is clearly no halting the bond that is growing between us." She looked deep into his eyes, pressed her nose into his neck and sucked in a deep breath. His intoxicating scent surrounded her, that of leather and spice and luxurious fur. In this moment, she had no desire to halt what was happening between them, the all-consuming need to be with her chosen one, to learn all she could about him, to know him as the man who held the other half of her soul. She wanted it all. She wanted him. "Come closer."

"As you wish." From over top of her, he ran his hands down her sides and along her hips, his cheek against her cheek as he nudged her head gently to one side and exposed her neck. Carefully, he nipped along her jawline and down the creamy slope of her skin until he reached the sensitive hollow where her neck and shoulder met. Her pulse pounded strongly, erratically, then hard and fast as he sucked her flesh into his mouth and released a low rumble. "I need to bite you, the way my shifter kind do with their chosen ones. Say aye, Lilias, because I can't do so until you give me your agreement."

"Aye, you have my agreement." Everything between them led toward a soul bound match that neither of them could ignore. She certainly couldn't. Pushing her hands deep into his silky hair, she scratched his scalp with her nails. "Mark me."

"I've been waiting to hear those two words for what feels like a lifetime." He clicked his fingers and her V-necked sweater disappeared and reappeared on the floor beside her. "I believe we have something in common."

"You can only apport clothing if you can see it."

"True, so be ready for me to apport the rest of your clothes off next. That's the only warning you're going to get." Head dipped, he buried his face between her breasts, her nipples pebbling tight and hard. He cupped one mound and latched his mouth over the beading nipple. Sucking hard, he made her moan, heat swelling outward from the sensitive bud.

"On my neck. I meant for you to mark me on my neck."

"I intend to mark you everywhere." Chuckling, he released her nipple and with his thumb, stroked over the thumping pulse point in her neck before sinking his teeth into the same spot.

She bucked on the floor and cried out as an intense wave of need washed through her.

Sweet heaven. His bite had curled her toes and now she had to bite him back.

She shoved against his shoulders, rolled them both over until she lay on top of him on the floor. Tongue out, she licked his neck and grazed her teeth over the spot.

"Bite me," he snapped as he arched into her, his decree

rough and demanding. "I need to be able to see the evidence of your mark on my skin."

"As you wish." With her heartbeat a fierce, thundering roar in her ears, she clamped down and stamped her mark on him. When she lifted her head, a large red spot bloomed, and she gently rubbed the mark of her possession with her thumb. "No one can miss seeing this."

"The mark I made on you is already fading." He stroked her neck.

"Well, we immortal heal quickly." She frowned as the mark she'd made on his neck began to disappear. "Oh, of course, shifters heal quickly too."

"Aye, far quicker than I currently wish to." He tipped her head to the side, razzed his teeth back and forth over her neck, then slowly, succinctly, he sank his teeth into her before flipping her back onto her back, his claws slicing out and digging into the floorboards.

This was the mated bond, one she desired with all her heart.

"Lilias?" A rap sounded on the door. "'Tis Cherub."

She shook her head and forced the sensual fog penetrating her mind to lift. Pulling back, she marshalled her thoughts and nudged Levi's shoulders. "Cherub's here."

"Pardon?" Eyes glazed, he slowly blinked.

"Excuse me," Cherub trilled. "Kirk and I are outside your door. We were supposed to meet in the inner bailey ten minutes ago but neither of you turned up. Thus, we are here now."

Another rap, this time Kirk's voice echoing through the wooden paneling. "We can smell your raging pheromones from out here, and we're not trying to torture you, but we need to leave for Dunvegan Castle since we're sailing and not driving. We've got to be there by this evening."

"I hate you both, but we're coming." Levi promptly pushed to his feet and held out his hand to her, murmured, "We'll resume our discussion later."

"We'd better." Smiling, she grasped his hand, got lifted to her feet, then waved a hand over her chest and the full length of his body as she reclothed them both. A quick step to the door and she opened it to Cherub and Kirk standing arm in arm before her. "I'll have you both know we're ready to leave even though you asked at a most inconvenient time."

"Definitely no' an innocent any longer. It could be time for that conversation now, my dear niece." Cherub caught her arm and walked with her along the hallway. "Where should I start?"

Chapter 7

Plunging his oars into the depths of the blackened water rippling with the reflection of the moon, Levi steered the skiff the last few feet toward Dunvegan Castle's sea-gate landing. For him and his kin, journeying across the water was always preferable to taking the roads, and they'd reached the MacLeod's stronghold in good time, the winds favorable as they'd kept an eye on the shoreline. Up ahead, the castle rose like a fortress, light glowing from torches positioned along the winding trail leading upward to the keep. Smoothly, Levi gave one last turn of the oar and slowly brought the skiff gently alongside the landing. Kirk bounded out and secured their vessel to the mooring post, and Cherub joined Lilias at the bow before linking arms and hopping up together onto the dock.

Lilias touched his mind. *"You're frowning."*

"I don't like it when you move away from me." She'd been seated in front of him the entire journey, within arm's reach.

"All I did was disembark."

"It feels like miles." He set the oars aside, jumped onto the landing next to her and taking a deep breath, slowed his chaotically beating heart. The moon, a vibrant golden-yellow, hung heavy and almost full in the sky. Tomorrow night would be the night of the full moon, a night when his very soul would tug voraciously toward his mate's. Damn it. They only had one more night to wait. One more blasted night that he might never survive to, not when his need for her raged as strongly as it did.

"You dinnae have long to wait. Stay the course, Levi." Kirk, as if reading his thoughts, thumped his shoulder. Dressed in a black leather vest donned over a blue tunic, his thick leather guards encasing his forearms and providing protection, Kirk had come fully armed just as he had, a sword strapped to his hip and daggers sheathed at his wrists.

"I was about to offer the same advice to Levi, my tempting bear." Cherub kissed Kirk's cheek, her white fur cloak flapping about the long skirts of her blue velvet gown. Casting a look at Levi, she added, "Remember Ailith's warning. Until she sees more with her visionary skill, we continue on the path that's been set."

"Will do." He also wouldn't forget Ailith's final words to him about Lilias. *You and Lilias must stay together.* Which meant he wouldn't be leaving Lilias's side.

"Wonderful, and so now I shall take to the skies and see what I can view from above." Cherub motioned to Lilias. "My dear, you take to the water and see if you can find any trace of the amulet at sea, or the selkies Flora saw from this landing. Either will do." A narrowing of her eyes.

"I also cannae help but wonder if they were Oadh and Roy. Aisling sent them to us in the Adonis Isles, so mayhap she also sent them here for the MacLeod's celebration day."

"To steal the amulet that Aisling wants us to find?" Lilias shook her head. "That makes no sense. Why would she have her sons do such a thing?"

"I agree, no sense at all, but seers see the bigger picture, understand that some things must be set amiss afore they can be righted again. There is a journey here for all involved, a journey, I fear, that will lead us astray afore we can return to the right path."

"I'll keep your words firm in my mind as I swim." Lilias waved a hand down her body, her jeans and loose sweater shimmering away, her clothing replaced by a sky-blue tunic that reached her knees. Preparing to dive, she stepped to the edge of the landing, her arms out as she launched from the dock, her body fully arched over the water, except she never hit the surface. Levi hadn't allowed it. He'd activated his skill, moved her from one position to another, so that she'd dived straight into his arms. She landed with an, "Oomph."

Chuckling, he settled her back on her feet. "Sorry about that, but Ailith said we must stay together. You taking to the water would go against her decree."

"My sister simply meant that we shouldnae be miles apart or separated by the realms. I willnae swim too far from the shore, no more than a few hundred feet."

"What if you get into trouble?" He pointed to the waves. "There are sharks out there."

"Levi, I have night vision and can see below the surface." Curling her arms around his neck, she rubbed up against him. "What is truly bothering you?"

"I'm not yet ready to lose sight of you." The truth, honest and raw. "There are whales out there too, large man-eating whales. They'd gobble you up whole. They'd surely know you'd be a tasty treat."

"They are gentle giants."

"What about all the stingrays? They have dangerous barbs."

"They are adorable. I love reaching out a hand as they glide past. They always present their underbellies for a rub." She stroked the side of his neck, right over the spot where she'd marked him earlier. "My adventurous bear, I will touch base with you now and then, although I do need to search these waters and I am the obvious choice. We cannae leave any stone unturned, or waterway unsearched, in our case."

"I'm not changing my mind." He rubbed his forehead against her forehead.

"You have no choice." She thrust her hands into his hair, tugged his head to hers and kissed him until his thoughts completely scattered. Scattered so hard, he didn't even process her next move until she was gone. She'd dipped out of his tight hold and dived, disappearing below the surface before he could keep her in his sight and apport her back. Without a firm image of her as she swam, he didn't have a hope of making her reappear.

"All will be well." Kirk slapped his back just as Cherub shimmered into thin air, her form naught but mist as she streamed up into the night sky and soared away toward the castle.

"How do you do it?" He wanted to kick off his boots

and dive into the sea, to follow his mate wherever she led.

"It takes patience and time to release the tight hold we want to keep on our chosen ones. Come on." Kirk led the way along the winding trail leading up the steps cut into the rocky incline.

Levi gave in and followed. As he walked, he scoped the walkway and the massive gray stone curtain wall protecting Dunvegan Castle where it sat high on the cliffside, its position one which had ensured in past centuries that the guardsmen patrolling Dunvegan's battlements could easily keep watch over anyone entering their waters. Such a fortified position, the landward embankment on the other side of the castle now linked to the land by an imposing bridge that provided access to the stronghold.

"In the report you gave me," he said to Kirk, "it stated that the amulet had been bestowed by Ula to the young daughter of Balloch MacLeod and had been held in clan MacLeod's possession since the early twelve-hundreds. But what was so special about Balloch's daughter, other than that she had close ties to Ula through her father? Exactly why did Ula choose to give her amulet to Sirena? There's something we're missing, information we don't yet have."

"Whoever Sirena was, she'll be naught but ashes now, nevertheless, we should ask Flora that question, see if she can give us some further information." Kirk frowned as they strode side by side. "I'd also like to know more about Balloch too."

"He'll be ashes as well. Long gone by now." Through a darkened passageway, Levi tramped with Kirk then passed into an inner courtyard where up ahead, the stone entry of the keep beckoned, light shining from the multitude of square windows along the upper floors.

Flora stood under the eaves in her red cardigan and white jeans. She waved to them from the front door just as a mist streamed high overhead and floated toward the landward side of the castle. Cherub. The fae princess was gliding around the castle in ever-widening circles.

"Levi." A whisper of his name from Lilias. *"Cherub hasnae seen anything of import as yet, so she is going to sweep toward the moors, take in a wider search grid."*

"Where are you?" Once they completed the bond, he'd be able to forge a merged link of the mind and reach her with ease, meaning he wouldn't have to wait for her to activate her telepathy.

"I'm searching every crevice along the seabed."

"Stay safe."

"You fret far too much. I am an immortal."

"I will always worry when you're away from my side, my sweet water nymph."

"There is no need for worry." She closed the link, and he released a feral growl.

So frustrating. Forcing his attention back to Flora, he extended a hand to her. "How was your drive home?"

"Likely not as enjoyable as your sail from the mainland. I love being out on the water, either sailing or swimming. There is such beauty below the surface of the sea." Smiling, she shook his offered hand, Kirk's too, her golden hair pulled into a high ponytail and her gaze hidden behind the darkened lenses of her glasses. She rocked onto her heels, looked over his shoulder toward the walkway they'd traversed. "Where are Cherub and Lilias?"

"They'll follow shortly." He flicked a look at Kirk. "Won't they?"

"Aye, the ladies will catch up soon enough. Will you show us inside, Flora?" Kirk opened the door for Flora.

"Of course. Come this way." Flora stepped inside, Kirk walking behind her while Levi took the rear.

They bypassed the great hall and continued toward the rooms housing Dunvegan Castle's artifacts. Up ahead, a plaque was affixed to the door, the plated tile inscribed with the word *Museum.* "You said you kept the Mother of Pearl housed in a safe in your father's solar?" Levi checked. "I'd like to see the safe."

"I'll show you."

"Lead the way then." Levi wandered past the displays in the museum, the walls painted a deep blue and the floorboards covered with an elegant Aubusson mat of blue, burgundy, and cream. Oak shelving held all manner of antique items.

He stopped next to an armoire and frowned at a deep gouge mark slashed into the side of the polished oak. It looked as if someone had been moving this piece of furniture about and hit it against something. Since Flora and Kirk had walked on without him, he carefully rubbed his palm over the damage and brought forth his ability.

Not only could he move articles by apporting them, but he could also transfer fibers about, like the fibers of this bookcase.

Focusing on the wood underneath his palm, he allowed heat to build in his body until a soft glow radiated out from his hand. The wooden fibers swelled and moved, then slowly settled before knitting back together right under his fingertips. When he lifted his hand from the wood, smoothness remained, not a mark in sight.

"Did you, ah..." Flora stared at him, at the armoire, then at him again.

Damn it. She and Kirk must have doubled back since he'd been taking so long.

"Oh my, how incredible." Plucking her glasses from her nose, Flora inspected the armoire with a gentle finger along the wood he'd fixed.

"I can explain." He'd better come up with something fast.

"There's no need." She pointed to the MacLeod Fairy Flag encased in a large frame on the wall, the crimson and yellow patterned silk flag, which had become discolored and aged over time, now dating back to the fourth century. "That flag represents my clan MacLeod fairy blood, a lineage that still flows strongly though my line. There are some within my clan who can do as you can. Mend things that can't be mended, that is, although not to the extent you just did, but still, I understand that sometimes there is magic where one least expects it."

"I hold the skill to apport," Levi admitted, which surprised him, since he'd never told anyone outside of his clan that information. "Gee, there's something about you, Flora, which makes me spill my guts."

She laughed. "What you did is extraordinary, and obviously, I'd never tell another soul about what I've seen you do. I have secrets of my own, can understand the need for keeping things quiet." Her eyes, no longer hidden by her glasses since she'd removed them, suddenly swirled, the misty blue-gray color of her irises becoming brighter.

Much brighter. The blue sparkled and outshone the gray, her eyes changing color again and becoming a living seascape.

Levi could actually see the sea taking form within her eyes, one wave rising and crashing over another.

She watched him and Kirk intently, her glasses in her hand and her eyes still displaying the stormy ocean vista. "You're not imagining it," she murmured. "What my eyes are doing, well, that's why I keep them concealed, and I'm not alone. There is one other whose eyes can reflect the sea just as mine do. It's time for me to lay out my own secrets, particularly if I want you to find the amulet."

"Who has eyes like yours?" Levi peered deeper into her eyes, mesmerized by them.

"Balloch's daughter, the lass named Sirena."

Stunned, he simply stared at her. "I, ah, why did a Siren of the Sea gift Balloch's daughter with such a powerful talisman? What was so special about her? Was it just her eyes then?"

"Nay, it was her parentage."

"Would you care to elaborate?" Levi edged a step closer, as did Kirk.

"I will, but first, there is something I must show you and Kirk in my father's solar, not just his safe, but another missing item." She walked toward a side antechamber and he and Kirk followed until they stood over a small redwood chest on the floor in the center of what was clearly Calder's private domain, the door to a large safe open along one wall.

The wind blew in the open window and fluttered papers on a desk.

"This is my father's solar where he tends to any administration matters for the keep." She lowered to a crouch and removed the engraved lid of the chest. Pressing one hand to the white satin lining of the strongbox, she continued, "I mentioned my sixth sense earlier, my seer lineage. I knew when you arrived that I'd have to show you this chest, and to apprise you of what was kept within it. A selkie skin. After my visit to Matheson Castle, I found this chest empty and the skin missing. I don't know who took it, other than that it wasn't one of my clansmen, or my father. It's gone missing, the same as the Mother of Pearl has."

"You had a selkie skin in your possession?" Levi's tongue got stuck to the roof of his mouth. "A real selkie skin?"

"Wait." Kirk shook his head in clear shock. "How did you come by a selkie skin?"

"That is a long story, but you can be assured I speak the truth. My father is away, high in the mountains of the Isle of Skye and won't be returning for at least another week. He has a sat phone but only turns it on when he needs to make a call, and I can't leave Dunvegan to inform him of the missing item, not when I'm needed here. I need you to tell him for me. Will you do that?"

"That shouldn't be a problem." Whatever she needed them to do, they'd do it. Lowering to his haunches next to Flora, he gently ran his hand along the inside of the chest's padded lining, the material holding smudge marks on it, along with a hint of seal fur. "Take a walk around the room, Kirk," he instructed his kinsman. "See if the thief has left a clue for us to follow."

"On it." Kirk looked inside the safe and checked each

shelf before heading to the desk then around to each corner of the room. A glance back at him, along with a shake of his head.

"Is anything else missing?" Levi asked Flora.

"Nothing else that I could tell." She took a deep, steadying breath. "For you to truly understand the ramifications of what's going on, with the loss of our amulet and now this selkie skin, I must place my full trust in you. I shall begin my story if you wish to hear it?"

"Aye, we do, otherwise we'll be walking blind in this case." A firm nod from Kirk.

"I sensed as much." She crossed to the desk, perched on one corner. "Centuries and centuries ago, a human druid warrior from clan MacLeod was walking along the shoreline of our land when he spied something extraordinary, a selkie gliding through the surf. Intrigued, he clambered up onto a rocky outcropping rising from one point of the bay to keep an eye on it, but as the druid warrior watched, the selkie shed its skin and showed itself to him. It was a woman. She had thick black hair and beautiful blue eyes. She stood in the moonlight, her gaze drawn to the druid warrior, except as he stepped closer, she became frightened and slid back into her skin before returning to the sea. A number of weeks passed, and on the night of the next full moon, the same druid warrior, who had trekked to the Druid Pool high in the mountains of the Isle of Skye, where my father currently is, once again came upon the same woman basking along the embankment. He'd found her again, but in a different place, and he could tell it was her by the color of her seal skin but wondered why on earth she'd come to the Druid Pool. Then she shed her skin and this time, without fear, walked to him. The druid warrior joined her, then without a word, he stripped off his clothes and weapons and dove into the water with her. She left her skin behind on the rocks, and they swam together under a waterfall rimming the pool. That is the place where over the months ahead, the two of them met in secret and fell in love. Her name was Aisling, and she was a selkie seer, her skill having *shown* her that the human druid warrior would be her one true love. That is why she sought him out, and why several months later when she gave birth to their son, a child born fully immortal with selkie, druid, and human blood, she knew that child would come to do great things."

"We've heard of the selkie seer Aisling." Kirk blew out a long breath. "What an incredible tale."

"It isn't just a tale. It's a fact." She nodded at them both. "Aisling adored her newborn son and watched him as he grew into adulthood, her child preferring to remain on Earth at his father's side rather than in the selkie realm. Her son, once he reached full maturity, chose to become a druid warrior as his father had been, having learned his craft at his father's knee. Many years later, when Aisling's son's father passed away, instead of leaving Dunvegan Castle to join Aisling in the selkie realm, he instead chose to remain here at this keep rather than take to the water. Aisling's son kept his selkie skin safe within this chest, using it only when his need for the water grew too strong."

"Does Aisling's son have a name?" Levi queried.

"Aye, he is the one called Balloch MacLeod, and he's an immortal, the last remaining druid warrior in his line, his daughter being Sirena, who is an immortal too, although both father and daughter have changed their names often over the centuries, in order for them to remain, without suspicion, on Earth."

"Who's Sirena's mother?"

"Ula, the first Siren of the Sea, and I, well, I am her daughter. I am Sirena, now known as Flora, my name having changed often over the centuries."

"Your parents are Ula and Balloch?"

"Aye, and my mama takes all care to keep my whereabouts a secret."

"We both know your father's name is Calder."

"Aye, Calder is the name Balloch chooses to go by in this era and time, while I go by Flora, and I am," she continued, "the only living being in all the realms who carries the blood of the sirens, the selkies, the druids, and of course, the humans who walk this Earth. That is why my eyes reflect the sea. That is why I shield them. That is why I am the holder of the Mother of Pearl, for the selkie seer Aisling is my grandmother, and she instructed my mama centuries ago, to gift me the amulet so I could keep it safe from Triton, who would try to use and abuse its power. Now, I need you to find it, for if you don't, I fear grave things will happen to us all."

Chapter 8

Levi sat in the water garden overlooking the loch only a short walk from Dunvegan Castle. He'd come here to try and clear his head after all he'd learned from Flora about her parentage, but so far, the fresh air hadn't made a dent in clearing his muddled thoughts.

Flora was an ancient being.

The daughter of Ula and Balloch, her father now known as Calder.

She held the ancestry of four strong bloodlines. A unique lineage.

She was one of a kind.

So many thoughts. Too many thoughts bombarded his mind.

Breathing deep, he tried to clear his head.

Leaning back against the garden bench, he spied a colorful goldfinch. It chirped then hopped along a branch before flying to the water fountain. The bird dipped its beak into the water for a drink, and the surface rippled with the wee creature's reflection. Its beautiful gold feathers were interspersed with blue-black tips, the bird's head banded with colors of vivid red, white, and blue-black.

The tiny bird hopped up onto a stony basin and splashed about before hopping back onto the edge. It preened its feathers, while on the other side of the fountain, he caught the scent of his mate on the nighttime breeze.

He bounded to his feet, strode past the fountain, and followed the pathway cutting through the trees toward another large garden holding a hidden oasis of ponds, all filled with water fed by the waterfalls that flowed down from the mountains of the Isle of Skye toward the sea.

Ducking around a leafy tree, he halted at the sight of Lilias seated on an elegant iron bench in a gauzy white silken gown that swept to her ankles, the fabric hugging her womanly curves and the golden light of the moon shimmering over her hair and setting the red strands ablaze. Lily pads floated within the pond before her.

Mouth dry, his tongue got stuck as he soaked in the sight of her.

Her long red locks swayed in soft curls to her lush bottom.

He cleared his throat, and she glanced up.

Her emerald eyes went wide as she pushed to her feet, bare feet with webbing between her toes. He'd never noticed that before, the webbing. She dug her toes into the lush grass springing up from around the stone-lined pond, clasped her hands behind her back and nibbled on her lower lip.

He moved toward her and halted within arm's reach.

As he looked into her eyes, time seemed to slow, his

thoughts becoming fully focused on her. "How'd your search of the seabed go?"

"'Twas a bust as you and those in your era would say." She wriggled her toes again, and he lowered to a crouch and eyed the intricate webbing. He wanted to trace the webbing, but she dug her toes even deeper into the grass.

Instead, he asked, "May I touch your scales?" She gave a silent nod, and he ran one finger along the line of shimmery pearl-colored scales covering her ankles and calves. She wobbled but managed to grasp his shoulders to hold herself steady. He slowly pushed to his feet and leaned into her ear, whispered, "The full moon is tomorrow eve, but I'm not sure I can make it. I want to ravish you tonight."

His mouth watered for a taste of her, his fingers itching as he palmed the beaded tips of her nipples poking through the thin white fabric of her gown. She wriggled her hips against his hips, her saucy move making his cock harden in his pants.

Head dipped, he kissed her, long and thoroughly as he delved into the sweetly warm recesses of her mouth, her soft body pressed against every inch of his and making him so damn hot.

She was the one he'd been waiting a lifetime for, and to have found his chosen one, a determined and devoted woman, was a blessing he'd never take lightly. Aye, his sweet water nymph was his match in every way, and he intended on showing her exactly how much he adored her.

His bear scratched deep inside him, clawing to get out, to ensure they both made sure she knew she was theirs.

A low growl rumbled up his throat and escaped his

lips. His claws sliced out and back in, his need for her becoming a feral necessity this close to the full moon.

"'Tis all right," she murmured in a soothing tone as she caught his hand and kissed his knuckles, his bear going instantly quiet at the contact before releasing a rumbling purr. "Your other half clearly likes it when I touch you."

"We both love it, need it. You've got to touch us more often, Lilias."

"Let's walk, hmmm?" She threaded her fingers through his and led him through the garden and up the steps into a gazebo with a turret-shaped roof and wooden seats rimming the perimeter. They sat, his outer thigh rubbing against her outer thigh.

Hell, he couldn't halt his need for more skin contact, the kind of contact that stated his claim. Tucking her hair back behind her ear, he gave no warning and simply sank his teeth into her neck, right over her thumping pulse.

She speared her fingers deep into his hair and held him close as he continued to nibble down her neck and along the upper swells of her breasts. Teeth scraping back and forth, he bit down again, and she released a soft sigh. "You are a handful, Levi Matheson."

"Aye, but I'm your handful."

"When we first met, we bickered and competed against each other." She lifted the medallion at her neck, twirled it between two fingers. "Now, all I want to do is wave one hand down your body and strip your clothes away, to never bicker again but instead make love."

"I wouldn't object." He nipped her neck one last time before lifting his gaze and looking into her eyes. The breeze rose, lifted strands of her red hair across her cheeks, and he caught a lock and curled it around his finger. Underneath the glow of the moon, her white satin gown draped far too provocatively across her nipples and caused the moon to highlight the pale pink of her areoles.

He wanted to rip her gown away, to touch the heated length of her skin. To lick her lips. To taste the scent of the sea on her flesh. To press a hand to her heart and feel the rapid beat under his palm.

His hunger grew fiercer, and her eyes widened, the gold flecks shimmering bright within the emerald depths.

"Levi, you need to cease looking at me the way you currently are. I dinnae think—"

"Perhaps we're both thinking too much. I want to complete the bond."

"I do too." She touched her nose to his nose.

"Then that's what we'll do." He crushed his mouth against her mouth and kissed her with all the fierce passion rising within him.

She tasted so incredibly delectable and so deliciously divine, like the ripest fruit dipped in the sweetest honey. He kissed her even deeper, until the exquisite taste of her swarmed his senses, then he yanked the gauzy neckline of her gown to one side and eased his hand inside, filled his palm with the warm flesh of her breast and released a throaty growl.

"Oh my, that feels…that feels…dinnae stop."

His cock jerked in his pants, a feral need taking over him.

He lifted her onto his lap, her legs straddling his legs, the hem of her gown split wide across her upper thighs and her sparkly scales glimmering on her lower limbs. He plunged his tongue inside her mouth and got drunk on the sweet nectar of her.

"Goodness, your kisses and your touch feel so divine." She grasped his face, a whimper escaping her lips as she moved her mouth over his mouth.

It was a losing battle to keep any of his remaining passion at bay, not when she wanted him in the same way he wanted her. Entwining his tongue with her tongue, he entered into a delicious dance with her, one that finally soothed a little of his rampaging need, yet also sent his need roaring higher.

"More," she whispered and clamped her knees over his hips. She rocked on his lap and aye, he'd give her more, her husky plea speaking to him.

He ripped her gown down one side, from neckline to waist. Perfect. Now he had more of her to feast on. Head dipped, he grazed his teeth over her nipple, her lush breasts taunting him to be even more wicked with her. A roll of his tongue around the peak then he drew her nipple deep inside his mouth and sucked hard.

"Levi." She moaned his name, her fingers stabbing into his shoulders, the heat of her core so close that his cock swelled painfully hard, the head escaping the waistband of his pants. "I want you to claim me."

He couldn't halt from gorging himself on her.

He lapped at her other breast, giving the tight bud equal attention, the warmth of her body pulsing with heat around him. He rubbed his chest against her breasts to better embed his scent into her, and to take her scent into his skin in return.

"Please, Levi. Dinnae stop kissing me." Her emerald

eyes glittered bright.

He scooped her bottom, squeezed her lower cheeks, her red locks cascading down her back like a river of rippling water, the ends sweeping across his knees.

She pulled the hem of his white shirt from his black jeans, then slid her hands underneath the soft cotton and explored. Gently, she caressed his torso, skimming his abdominal muscles and running her fingers over the muscles along the sides of his body. She looked into his eyes, the hope in her own eyes making his hope rise. They would complete the bond now. She would be his, and he would be hers.

Desperation roared through him, his jaw aching as he craved the need to sink his teeth into the soft flesh at her neck once again. He'd mark her over and over. Even his bear pushed for the same, and she smiled, swept her fingers in small circles over his middle and gave his bear more of her attention.

"Your bear is talking to me, Levi." Her smile widened. "Will you bring him out?"

"Not right now. He's on the cusp of insanity with the full moon this close, would certainly take a massive bite out of you. A bite that wouldn't even compare to my wee nips this night."

With a stuttered breath, she stripped his shirt off and dropped it onto the bench before gliding her hands over his pecs. "I want to touch you," she demanded. "The same way you're currently touching me."

She was offering him more skin-on-skin contact.

He desperately wanted it.

He grasped her lush bottom in his hands and when she

licked her lips, he couldn't help but follow the sweet telling action of her tongue with his gaze. She left her lips wet and plump.

"We really need a bed," he croaked. "I'd apport my waterbed, except the distance is too great. It would probably end up sinking into the sea somewhere between here and Matheson Castle."

She tapped his lips with one finger, her own lips lifting in a heavenly smile. "We dinnae need a bed, just each other."

"I love the way you think."

Chapter 9

A deep, raw need made Lilias's breasts swell, her nipples beyond sensitive. She rubbed her breasts against Levi's bare chest. Back and forth. Back and forth, until the peaked tips tingled, and every inch of her upper body got coated in his masculine scent, his skin so blazingly hot against her skin. She'd never experienced a more insane desire, or a more magical place to allow that desire to escalate. She sat in a beautiful gazebo with her chosen one, the fountains all around gurgling water and the pools rippling under the moonlight, birds splashing about, and the sweet sound of the crashing waves reaching her on the breeze from Loch Dunvegan.

A husky rumble vibrated in her mate's chest, the rumble causing a fierce heat to gather in her middle and flare down between her thighs. She struggled for a breath and so did he, this moment under the midnight moon the most sublime of her life.

Arms hooked around his neck, she leaned her head

back, her gaze on the twinkling stars shining through the open domed beams of the pergola, the golden orb of the moon so close to its fullest. Just one more night and it would reach its peak. She kept her neck angled toward her chosen one in the hope he'd bite her again, and she gasped as he closed his mouth over her neck. He scraped his teeth downward then licked back up along the same spot. He was so close to sinking his teeth into her. He just needed one more push. "Do it," she whispered.

"You already have my mark," he teased before capturing her mouth with his. He swept his tongue inside and licked across her tongue.

Such intense pleasure radiated through her, his kiss so fierce yet also so tender. Squirming on his lap, she fisted her hands in his hair. His scent was intoxicating, a wonderful mix of leather and spice and all things nice.

She broke their kiss and dipped her head to his neck. Since he wasn't going to bite her, she intended on having a little nibble on him instead. She trailed her lips over his pounding pulse point and licked while he groaned and clutched her bottom harder.

"Levi, Lilias!" A shout sounded from somewhere along the pathway leading to the pergola, Kirk's voice somehow invading the fog engulfing her head.

She straightened and struggled to right her breathing as she caught not one set of footsteps but two. "Cherub and Kirk are coming," she whispered to Levi. "Goodness, but they have the worst timing."

"I think they're trying to kill us." Levi traced one finger along her lower lip, his gaze dipping to her ripped gown. "I want to devour you."

"Levi, Lilias!" Another shout from Kirk.

"Here," she called back and regrettably scuttled from Levi's lap. With one wave down her body, she clothed herself in a regal floral gown accented with frilly lace along the neckline of the cinched bodice and the edges of the long, draping sleeves. She left her feet bare. "Do you need a hand?"

"I've got this." He snagged his white shirt from the bench and tugged it over his head before tucking the hem into his black jeans, the hilt of his belted sword gleaming from his right hip. He gently pushed his fingers through her hair and tidied her locks, then caught her hand and linked their fingers together.

He jogged down the steps of the pergola and strode along the pathway to where Kirk and Cherub emerged around a garden overflowing with ferns and greenery. Bright yellow, red, and white flowers waved their heads from within the garden bed.

Kirk gave her a smile and a wink. "I thought if I followed Levi's scent it would lead me to both of you. Flora has laid out tea and cake in the library and prepared rooms for us. How was your search of the loch?"

"I found naught other than several rusty tins, a few nails, and an old ship's anchor." She clasped her aunt's hand. "How did your search of the surrounding terrain transpire?"

"I too found naught amiss, although when Kirk updated me on Flora's heritage and her father's missing selkie skin, I couldnae believe what I heard."

"Pardon?" Her mouth gaped open.

"My apologies." Levi slapped his forehead, mumbled,

"I haven't had the chance to update Lilias on all of that yet."

"What heritage?" She spun on her mate. "How does Flora's father have a selkie skin?" She'd missed so much, had been so consumed by him that she'd completely forgotten all about their mission.

"Well, long story short," Levi stated, his brow furrowing. "Centuries ago, a human druid warrior from clan MacLeod fell in love with a selkie seer named Aisling. She gave birth to their son, the child born fully immortal with selkie, druid, and human blood. That son, known as Balloch, has always kept his selkie skin safe within a chest in Dunvegan Castle. Once he reached adulthood, Balloch went on and joined with Ula, and the two of them became parents to a daughter named Sirena. Their daughter was born an immortal too, and holds siren, selkie, druid, and human blood."

"So that's why Ula actually gifted her amulet to Balloch's daughter, because his daughter was her daughter too." She slapped her leg. That finally made sense. "Although I didnae know Aisling had a third son, one in addition to Oadh and Roy. She's never spoken of Balloch, nor have Oadh and Roy."

"There's more yet." Levi grasped her shoulder. "Balloch, Aisling's son, changed his name often over the years, his daughter doing the same. Balloch is actually Calder, and Sirena is Flora."

"I beg your pardon?" More shock. "I didnae expect you to say that. How intriguing."

"Obviously, we can't speak of this to another, Calder and Flora's secrets theirs to keep."

"Of course." She'd never utter a word to another, understood the need for secrecy well. Facing Cherub, she eyed her aunt. "You said Kirk updated you on Flora's heritage and her father's missing selkie skin. How did Balloch, I mean Calder, lose his selkie skin?"

"He didnae lose it. 'Tis been taken and we dinnae know by whom." An imploring look from Cherub. "Flora has asked us to find both her amulet and her father's selkie skin, which of course we shall, for both items."

"I wish I could reach Ula telepathically." Lilias tapped her head in frustration. "Let her know that I've now learned the truth about her daughter, except I've never been able to reach her or any of the merpeople telepathically. They're able to block their minds."

"Then we must continue with our current path, the one set by Ailith in her vision." Firm words from her aunt.

"You're right, of course, you're right." Lilias continued along the path toward the keep, the four of them walking side by side, the solid warmth of her kin always present, and now her chosen one's too.

"We can't lose focus on our own mission while we aid Flora and Calder." Kirk adjusted the strap on his leather gauntleted wrist. "We need to remember the water fae and the changes you're going through. We can't allow Triton to keep Breena any longer than necessary. Finding her is imperative."

"Aye," Cherub agreed.

Levi squeezed Lilias's hand "We'll also find a way to halt the tails being forced upon you and the water fae by Triton."

"I'm not sure I'd say forced anymore." Her new tail

propelled her through the deep blue with far more speed than her legs ever had. "I have to admit, I enjoy being able to swim faster."

"I'm not surprised." He cocked a brow. "Except you should be able to control any shift, and since you can't, it is a burden you shouldn't have to deal with."

"Aye, not being able to choose when my tail appears is frustrating." She crossed a bridge with her kin then headed toward the front door of the keep, the moon casting a soft yellow glow over the cobbles. A Scottish flag flapped in the breeze from atop Dunvegan's turreted battlements, while ivy trailed up the walls toward a balcony jutting out from a long row of tall, narrow windows. Right above the eaves of the front door, a red light blinked from a camera and Cherub pulled the hood of her white fur cape over her head to hide her glittery skin before reaching the camera's range.

Kirk opened the door, and they entered the keep lit by ornate wall mounted lamps and overhead lights. "This is the way to the library," he called with a wave of one hand as he jogged up the ornate wide wooden staircase.

Lilias lifted her skirts as she walked behind Cherub, her bare feet warmed by the wool of the burgundy runner. They continued along a passageway lined with portraits of the past Chiefs of Clan MacLeod, the library doors up ahead open in welcome. She walked into the tastefully furnished library holding dark wooden shelves and leather-bound tomes. Row after row of bookshelves reached all the way to the vaulted ceiling, the large room lit by corner lamps and high light fixtures with a fire roaring in the hearth. A thickly padded burgundy settee and two armchairs were positioned to one side, so people could sit and enjoy the warmth of the fire as they read.

"Cherub, Lilias, welcome to Dunvegan Castle." Flora rose from a chair in front of the library desk, set a pen down and wandered toward them, her jean-clad legs covered, her feet encased in thick woolen slipper socks, any scales hidden from sight, and she must surely have scales since her mother was Ula.

Lilias couldn't keep her curiosity at bay a moment longer. "Flora, Levi and Kirk have updated Cherub and me about everything. You have shared so much, yet I have no' had the chance to be honest with you."

"You'd like to share something?" Flora removed her glasses, her eyes a misty blue gray that reflected the waves of the sea, nay, not reflect. Her eyes began to sparkle and *become* the sea, as if one wave were crashing over another within her eyes.

"Your eyes are so beautiful." Lilias stumbled a step closer, drawn into them. "They make me long to take a dip in the ocean."

"They are a reflection of my unique blood."

"So fascinating." She didn't want to miss a moment of the magic of the sea coming to life within Flora's eyes, couldn't help but grasp Flora's shoulders and sink closer toward her. "Stunning."

"Speaking of unique blood." Cherub pushed back her hood.

"Oh my." Flora clapped a hand over her mouth, uttered, "You have sparkly skin."

"I'm the eldest child born to Ailbert, King of the Fae, gifted with this skin which marks the firstborn within our royal line. I'm also a time-walker and hold the ability to open portals and travel through the centuries as needed. You may be unique, Flora, but so am I, and so is Lilias. Lilias is one of the water fae. She can breathe underwater just as the sirens do. You'll never be alone again, not now we know who you are."

"Incredible." Flora's face had gone pale but now pink suffused her cheeks. "I have another admission. I'm friends with one of the water fae, secretly, of course."

"Who?" Lilias asked her.

"Breena." Flora's eyes continued to dance with the sea. "Breena is one of only a handful of people who know my true heritage. She and Ula have always been close confidants, and during my childhood, Ula asked Breena to teach me how to navigate the deep blue here on Earth. My mama couldn't always see to my instruction since Triton often tried to follow her as she swam between the realms." Flora rolled one of her socks down and lifted the hem of her jeans higher. Scales glittered on her calves.

"Breena kept your secret, has never spoken a word about you to any of my fellow fae." Lilias lifted her skirts to her knees and showed her own scales. "These scales appeared on the water fae's legs not long after Triton abducted Breena. He spoke a spell over her, and now we're trying to find her. That's why we want to help you find your amulet. We need to borrow it before we return it to you."

"But Cherub can open a portal." Flora glanced at Cherub. "You just said you're a time-walker."

"I can only open portals to places that I can lock down the image for. Unfortunately, I have never located the exact whereabouts of Triton's lair, dinnae hold an image of it."

"My father's been there. He could show you how to get to Triton's lair."

"How do we find him?" Cherub's voice rang with need. "Of course, we've had our hearts set on finding your amulet, but if Triton can take us there, finding him might be the quickest route to get to Breena."

"He's at the Druid Pool high in the mountains, although you'll never be able to find it in the dark, will need to wait until first light. I have a map, a rather rudimentary one, but a map all the same." Flora hurried to the library ladder and pushed it along the polished floorboards to a section near the back. She climbed the ladder, retrieved a black leatherbound book with a single red ruby embedded in the spine. Returning to them, she opened the tome and presented a map.

"Let me take a look at that." Levi eyed the map, noted the route and pathways.

"You'll need to rest well this night before you begin the trek. It's a long, long walk from Dunvegan Castle." Flora glanced at each of them. "Rooms have been prepared down the hallway on your left. Please, could we meet for breakfast and talk some more before you leave?"

"Of course, we can, and you have our thanks for showing us this map." Lilias hugged Flora, and Cherub joined them in their hug, squeezed them both tight, and after a few more words between them, Flora left the library for her own bed with the promise that they'd talk again in the morning before they left for the Druid Pool.

Cherub and Kirk said their goodnights and departed for bed too, leaving just her and Levi alone in the library.

Completely enthralled by the huge number of tomes in the library, she climbed the ladder and nudged herself along the upper row, the ladder's wheels softly whirring as she slid across the polished floorboards, Levi walking with her, his hand curved around her ankle.

She searched along the rows and selected a tome which took her interest, the leather binding cracked along the spine. Carefully, she opened it to the first page, the paper yellowed with age, the title recorded as *The True Story of the Kelpies*.

"What have you found?" he asked, one eyebrow raised.

"Some light reading afore bedtime." She passed him the tome then pushed against the heavy oak of the bookshelf and sent the ladder gliding another few feet.

"Come and grab a bite. There's tea and cake that no one's touched." Levi seized her waist and lifted her free of the ladder, then with one hand at her lower back, he steered her toward the settee and the warmth of the crackling fire. He handed her a plate with lemon cake and sat down beside her with his own plate and bit into his slice. "Even though I had envisioned this night ending with us completing the bond, clearly dawn will be here in a matter of hours, and we have a long trek ahead of us tomorrow. I think we should wait."

"I think we should too." She couldn't help but smile as she bit into her slice of cake. "I'd also guarantee the moment we started kissing, Cherub and Kirk would be knocking on the door."

"Aye, I swear they've got a radar on us." He brought her hand to his lips and gently kissed the softness of her palm, then took her hand and pushed her fingers into his dark locks. "Use your nails and scratch my head."

"Pardon?"

"Shifters need touch in a way that soothes our bear, and currently my bear is feeling both tired and frustrated, which means he wants a hard scratch."

"Then I shall attempt to soothe your frustration." In the muted light of the library, the fire burning lower in the hearth, she slowly scratched his scalp, and he closed his eyes on a growly moan. She grinned, warmth heating her from deep inside and radiating out. She scratched him harder, her nails digging in, his silky hair a mix of dark brown and golden brown.

"Don't stop." One fiercely tender rumble.

"As you wish." She curled her hands around his nape and rubbed his neck with a gentle massage, then pushed her fingers underneath the neckline of his shirt.

"Let's rest. We've both had a long couple of days." He toppled her underneath him on the settee, and she rubbed her legs against the soft denim of his jeans.

"Do you want to make this our bed for the night?"

"Aye, I do."

"Then that's what we'll do." Looking deep into his magical shifter eyes, she got lost in the swirling golden color. Never had she felt this adored, this protected and cared for. Relaxing her head against his chest, she closed her eyes and drifted, the warmth of his embrace soothing her into a deep, delicious sleep.

Chapter 10 – Ula, Siren of the Sea

Her soul belongs to her sisters.
Her soul belongs to the sea.
Her soul reaches out from another world.
One of wonder and renewal.
One of power and sacred bloodlines.
Far away across the divide of realms…
Is where Ula, the Siren of the Sea, bides her time.

Near Triton's lair, Adonis Isles, after midnight.

Streaky black clouds hazed the night sky, allowing only a mere trace of moonlight to shine through as Ula swam toward Triton's underwater lair at the edge of a small atoll.

She'd received word from King Atlas that his half-brother had chosen to fight the punishment handed to him by Poseidon and had discovered a way to circumvent his sentence. Triton intended on outwitting his father by transferring his curse to another of his tailed kind, by way of capturing their tears and never spilling them.

On her way here to speak to Triton, she'd also come across Oadh and Roy, who'd been sent by Aisling to warn her about Triton kidnapping Breena, dear, sweet Breena. Aisling had *seen* that Triton had spoken a spell over her so that she'd forge a tail when wet. Except not only had that spell changed Breena, but it had also changed her fellow water fae.

Fury tore through Ula.

Triton had gone too far, had now hurt one of her dearest friends.

She'd fight for Breena's freedom, for all of the water fae's freedom.

Diving, she swam deep down through the waters to the place where a lower tunnel to Triton's cavern could be found. She and Calder had come here a time or two when dealing with Triton. They'd kept their visits short, just long enough to warn Triton away from interfering in their lives, not that Triton ever had. Their visits had only spurred Triton on.

Nearer, she kicked, and there, she spied the entrance among the barnacle encrusted rocks, the opening a jagged slit just wide enough for one of her tailed kind to pass through. She edged closer. Crabs scuttled out of her way while a sea snake slithered along the seabed. No time to delay. She grasped the edges of the slit and eased through, the tunnel widening a little from that point on. Swishing her tail, she passed through a craggy void, the water getting warmer as she followed the passageway leading upward.

She'd come alone today, even though three of her

sister sirens had demanded they join her on this mission, but in the past whenever Triton had seized one of them, he'd used their capture to hurt them all.

'Twas his battle strategy, so for that reason alone, and to remain undetected for as long as possible, 'twas agreed that only one of them would attempt to infiltrate Triton's lair. Her.

Fully armed, a lethal blade strapped to her back in a scabbard and dirks slotted at her wrists, she firmed her resolve and surged through the passageway. Moments later, she emerged within a hot pool of water surrounded by black rock walls that hissed with steam. 'Twas hotter than Hades in here, water lapping along the edge of the black sand of the cavern. Torches flickered along the walls, and there, an iron-barred cage sat half under and half above the water.

Breena splashed about in the shallows of the cell. Breena with a tail.

Gritting her teeth, she swam to Breena and grasped the bars where a chunky lock dangled from the door, a magical protective aura of red wrapped around it, the keyhole shimmering a crystal black color. Triton must have spelled the lock in addition to weaving an incantation over the key slot. She tugged and the chain clanked. "I'll free you soon, Breena."

"The lock is impenetrable." Breena reached through the bars and clutched her hands. "He's after all of the water fae, Ula, wishes to force a tail on us and create his very own new race of merpeople. Once he has my tears in a secure vial, he'll use me to ensure my kin abide by his wishes. He willnae halt his madness until he reigns supreme over us all."

"Spelled lock or no', I'll bust this lock open." She stuck her sword inside the lock and yanked. The chain and lock swayed but didn't crack. Huffing, she kept at it. "Tell me, did you hear the spell which created your tail?"

"Aye, 'twas an unforgiving one. He thought on it well afore administering it. He spelled my tail into being for each of those who hold my water ability, thirty water fae in all." Breena rattled the bars. "Ula, he also took away my ability to telepathically reach my kind, and for them to reach me. You cannae break this lock. Instead, you must find Lilias. Tell her where I am, and she will bring reinforcements to free me." Breena's face got redder, steam pluming. "The spell Triton spoke is linked to his life, so it can only be broken once he ceases to breathe."

"I have no issue slicing his head from his shoulders."

"You must take all care. We all must." Water bubbled around Breena, and she caught her breath, rose higher against the tide of heat, her tail curled against the bars. "Your sword is about to snap in two."

Breena was right.

"Swim fast, my friend." Breena grasped her hand through the bars, her gaze imploring.

"I shall." With no choice left, she dived toward the tunnel entrance.

The fastest way to find Lilias, since Lilias traveled often across the ages and realms, was to use her daughter's amulet to wish her way to her. She needed to get to Dunvegan Castle and find Flora first, ask her daughter to open Calder's safe and give her the amulet.

An hour later, she neared the closest gateway portal

within the Adonis Isles, her night vision illuminating the white of the arch. She pressed the glyphs that would allow her to travel through time to the seabed portal in the waters near Dunvegan Castle. Her heart ached, as it always did whenever she readied herself for travel to her daughter, the child she and Calder adored.

The chevron moved, locked onto the glyph, and she swished back and waited as the waves stirred. A massive funnel of water shoved outward then sucked back inward. She swam through the arch and got thrust through the darkness. Time spun as she got twisted about, and in a tangle of head-over-tail, she burst through the other end of the portal into the Western Isles.

She kicked to the surface and emerged where white-tipped waves crashed all around her, the night sky a velvety midnight blue. Her child was close. She kicked past the headland of the Isle of Skye toward Dunvegan Castle and halted as a deep pulse struck her heart.

She clutched her chest. The amulet had always called to her, from the moment she'd received it from the Tuath Dé, until the moment she'd gifted it to her daughter. Scooping water at her sides, she searched the seabed as she swam.

She squeezed her eyes shut, opened them again.

Down deep, she dived, then swam along the seafloor until the pulsing grew into a boom inside her chest, and there, washing back and forth in the undercurrent, her Celtic amulet sparkled in the crack between two rocks. How on earth had it ended up here?

She curled her hand around it, brought the precious keepsake to her heart. Mayhap Flora had lost it while out swimming, although that had never happened before, not when her daughter always took all care with it.

Carefully, she fastened the charm around her neck, then made her wish and called forth Lilias's name. There was no time to delay. She needed to reach her so they could rescue Breena.

A whirlpool opened and she kicked toward it.

The waves sucked her under.

A huge surge carried her away.

Kicking, she propelled herself forward through the portal as streams of water and wind breezed past, then she got shoved upward toward the surface.

Searching the sea, she waited as the whirlpool calmed, although she caught no sight of Lilias nearby. She growled under her breath, slapped the surface hard and water sprayed. She'd made a mistake. She'd been to this place before, an endless ocean that led nowhere. No Man's Sea. She'd been taken to the place in between the realms.

Aye, there was one stipulation when using the amulet.

One couldnae wish their way to whomever they desired when that person was desired more strongly by another. The last time such a thing had happened was when she'd used the amulet to wish her way to Mary, one of her sister sirens, although Mary had been honeymooning with her human lover at the time. She'd had to wait in between the realms for three days until Mary had returned to the water alone without her lover.

Whoever Lilias was with, until Lilias returned to the water without him, she'd have to wait here in No Man's Sea, unable to see to Breena's request. Unable to aid her dearest friend.

Frustration boiled inside her.

Chapter 11

On the comfortable settee, Lilias stirred from her sleep, the stars still twinkling out the library window, although dawn appeared close, the sky lightening a little. She went to move, discovered the blazing warmth at her back came from Levi, his muscled body curled protectively around hers, his arm draped over her hip and his forehead pressed against the back of her head, his slow and steady breaths stirring tendrils of her hair across her cheek.

She'd never awoken with such a sense of rightness and peace before.

For fear of waking him, she remained quiet, the last glowing embers in the fire dying out. She didn't want to move, didn't want this night to end.

"Hmm, need you closer," he rumbled as he stretched and rubbed against her.

Butterflies took flight in her middle. She caught his hand and lifted it from her hip and threaded their fingers together.

As the dawn sun breached the horizon, it sent a glorious spear of golden light across the room. She pressed his palm against her racing heartbeat, which had him releasing a soft, sensual sigh that vibrated against her back.

Oh, she had a sinfully sexy mate.

Wriggling her bottom against his crotch, she got a delightful surprise as his manhood poked into her, his length thick and hard and unable to be ignored. Slowly, carefully, she released his hand and rolled over until she faced him on the plush burgundy padding. Winding her arms around his neck, she smiled as he blinked his eyes open.

"Good morn, my chosen one." She touched her lips to the tip of his nose then pulled back, just a little. Not too far.

"Good morning to you too." He played with the lace adorning the neckline of her cinched bodice, one hand smoothing down her leg and rucking up the soft fabric of her white floral gown.

A ripple of delicious shivers fluttered up her spine, the desire she saw in his eyes flaring hot and strong.

He sliced out one claw, slit her bodice in two from her neck to her waist, then gripped the sides and ripped the remaining length of her skirts away, her body completely bared to his sight. "You're not wearing any undergarments."

"I rarely do."

"How am I supposed to wait until the full moon tonight before we complete the bond?" He brushed his fingers over the golden curls covering her mound.

"I could be persuaded to complete it now." She lifted the hem of his tight white shirt and swept it over his head, his chest a hard expanse of muscle she wanted to sink her teeth into.

"We're supposed to be meeting Cherub and Kirk and Flora in the dining room for breakfast."

"Then they'll have to wait for us. Touch me." She shivered with need.

"Aye, I need to touch you." Gently, he skimmed his middle finger through her curls and rubbed her nub.

She gasped as he stroked past the bundle of nerves and pushed deep into her heated center. She couldn't hold back her moan, nor halt her back from arching as he added a second finger and began spreading them deep inside her channel. Her inner flesh tightened around his fingers, her breath hitching.

Another moan, her bottom sliding off the settee.

She seized his shoulders, barely holding on. "We're going to end up on the cold, hard floorboards."

"No floorboards for my mate. My vote is for the large, padded desktop." He launched to his feet, gripped her butt in his hands and carried her to the wide library desk. With one sweep of his hand, he pushed the books and papers to the floor then leaning over her, he lowered her nude body onto the red leather pad covering the desktop and slid his fingers back inside her.

"The door," she murmured.

"Got it." He waved one hand and the lock clicked shut. "It's child's play to apport the locking mechanism into place." Nuzzling her neck, he kept pumping his fingers into her channel, and she popped the dome on his jeans and worked the zipper down.

She didn't want to leave this room. She wanted to

remain right here with him, her legs spread, her skin hot and her body open to his. A shocking insight. One that hit her deep in her heart. "I crave more time with you."

"As the full moon rises tonight, that craving will only grow for both of us."

"Make me yours." She looked deep into his eyes. "Right now, right here."

"I can't hold back another moment. Are you certain?" Whispered words in her ear, his fingers curling into a spot that had her back arching off the desk.

"Aye, very certain."

"Good answer." Grinning, his lips lifted so wickedly. "Let me bring you pleasure."

"You already are." With another curl of his fingers, another pump deep inside her, she could barely hold on. She grasped the edge of the desk, his caresses sending a molten wave of pressure rippling through her inner core. She shuddered, her knees going limp as her channel clung to his fingers. A cry tore from her lips as she clamped onto him.

"That's it, my sweet water nymph," he murmured with a nip of her lips.

"Oh, please, please…" She couldn't remain still, her head thrashing from side to side as an orgasm took a fierce hold of her.

"Please what?" he teased as teeth bared, he bit her neck and scraped down over her frantic pulse point.

"Everything. Please give me everything, Levi."

"You want me inside you?"

"Aye, for you to complete the bond and forge the merged link of the mind with me, just as your shifter kind do." She waved a hand and sent what remained of his clothes flickering away. His golden skin gleamed and his manhood jutted high from the nest of dark curls at his groin. "I cannae put into words how deeply I feel about you, but I intend on trying. Your touch is the only touch I crave, Levi. It always will be, because I know you are my chosen one, the man who holds the other half of my soul. I want you to take me and make me yours, for now and for all time."

"I want the same. Be prepared to reach the stars. I'm going to make you fly."

Chapter 12

From the moment Levi had awoken to the warmth of Lilias in his arms, her soft, sexy aroma filling his lungs, he'd never felt so needy and content all at once. Breathing deep, he drew in her sweet, mind-bending, sensuous scent, until a fog of need drifted over him, a need so strong his bear was on the brink of pushing forth to take full control. His bear wanted out, to take charge and claim her, just the same as he did.

He licked his lips at the sight of her nude body displayed so openly for him. He'd slashed her pretty gown to pieces, had laid her out on the desk, had pushed two fingers deep inside her until she'd coated him in her essence.

With her soft, creamy skin flushed from her orgasm, he lowered his head and licked between her breasts and around each mound until she arched her back and thrust her breasts even deeper into his roaming mouth. Such exquisite mounds. He clamped his mouth over one nipple and sucked hard, his chin brushing the undersides of her breasts. She tasted magical, as if her flesh held an elixir that had been prepared just for him, an elixir that sent his head spinning.

Half crazed with need, he lifted his head and took her mouth in his and kissed her with all the fierce passion exploding through him. She had driven him crazy with her warm breath whispering seductively over his tongue. This moment was sheer heaven.

"More," she whimpered against his lips, her hands fluttering over his shoulders.

"Aye, I'll give you more." He flipped her over onto her belly on the desk and she squealed at his fast move. "Stay still, because both my bear and I intend to take you the way that we need to."

"Oh my." She gasped for air, her breathing coming harder and faster, her emerald eyes ablaze with desire as she glanced over her shoulder at him.

Everything about his mate called to him, from the fierce way she looked at him to the way she wriggled her bottom and enticed him to take more.

Burning to take her, he pushed his nose into her hair, his mouth watering at the tasty sight of the long curve of her neck on display.

His cock got thicker and rose higher as he crowded her from behind, his chest fitting close against her back as he gripped the head of his throbbing shaft. "Are you ready for me?"

"Aye, you've made me more than ready." She smiled back at him, gave him a saucy wink. "Make us one."

"I can't go slow." There wasn't a chance, so he opened her folds and stroked the weeping head of his shaft along her slit, his teeth scraping along her neck as he did.

With a muttered curse, he sank deep, his cock pushing through her barrier until he filled her up. She drew in a fast breath, let out a low and needy moan. Need that slammed hard into him too, and before either of them could draw in their next breath, he pulled back and plunged balls-deep inside her.

He pumped hard, his mind surging into hers and tunneling deep. Bright sparks flared along the new and vibrant pathway between their minds as he created the merged link between a mated pair, the pathway sizzling with a heated blaze of gold and red. He fused the link into place, and she panted as he spoke along the private pathway between their minds. *"I no longer have to rely on your ability to reach me telepathically. I can find you at any time on my own."*

Cementing the link within her mind, she whispered along it, *"Aye, you can, and now we are exactly where we both belong, joined together in the way of a mated pair. You are my chosen one, Levi, mine and only mine."*

"You hold the other half of my soul, are now mated to a bear."

"I can handle your bear, provided you can handle being mated to a mermaid."

"It'll be as easy as a swim in the sea." He pounded into her and as he did, he nipped the skin of her neck and sucked it deep between his lips. *Bite her harder*, his bear demanded. He filled her up, his cock so damn hard that he couldn't hold on much longer. Except he wanted to send her careening to the stars once more, right along with him, and he wanted to do it looking into her eyes.

He slid an arm around her waist, lifted her from the desk and walked with her across to the white woolen mat in front of the fire.

Lowering her onto the plush mat, he plunged back inside her, one finger on her clit as he increased his pace. *"Bite me at the same time as I bite you."* Words he spoke huskily along their newly forged link.

"I'm going to do more than bite you, Levi Matheson. I'm going to speak the spell to ensure we're never separated again. When I do, I'll be taking your essence into my keeping, so that for as long as I live, so too shall you. We shall be the same as Cherub is with Kirk, and my sisters with their mates."

"Do it." Kirk, Hunter, and Liam had become immortal upon joining with their chosen ones, and even though Levi had never asked them exactly how that had occurred, he'd had a gut feeling it would be like this, when they were joined together as one.

He opened his mouth, bit down on her neck and she cupped the back of his head and sank her teeth into the same spot on his neck. Such tortuously sweet sensations thrummed through his body. A burning heat sizzled at the base of his spine and blazed around to his cock.

He plunged into her, over and over, and she lifted her hips and met each of his thrusts with the same fierce need that took him.

He pumped, and her channel tightened, her desire pinnacling as she squeezed his cock ruthlessly. Bellowing, he lost all control, his essence shooting from him in one long, hot spurt. His seed coated her womb and she bit him again before flying with him over the edge, her thoughts swirling greedily in and around his own.

Extreme heat and roaring pleasure ignited along their merged link, her channel pulsing around his cock with a possessive pull.

Grasping his face between her hands, she looked deep into his eyes and spoke out loud, "From this moment forward, I hereby bind Levi Matheson's soul to mine. Give me a piece of his inner light so that I might guide and watch over him, throughout all of time. He is mine, just as I am his."

A sizzling light shimmered from around his body, lighting up the white rug underneath them. Tendrils separated from his body and glided toward her. She opened her mouth, breathed them inside her body and allowed the merging of their hearts, bodies, and souls. "Amazing," he whispered.

"'Tis done, Levi. Welcome to the world of the immortal fae."

"Well, clearly you can't get rid of me now even if you wanted to." Grinning, he kissed her again, his mind and body locked tight around hers.

He'd never experienced such a moment of absolute perfection, but he intended to experience it again, over and over, for all the centuries to come. Peace and joy assailed him.

Chapter 13

Lilias stepped outside into the early morning sunshine along with Levi, her body still humming from the delicious joining with her chosen one. Levi eased in behind her, settled his hands on her hips, his wonderful leather and spice aroma wrapping fully around her. He rubbed his body against hers and she laughed as she looked over her shoulder at him. "Is your bear embedding more of his scent into me?"

"Aye, he's feeling very territorial about you." He nuzzled her neck, the loose white tunic she'd clothed him in tucked into a belted kilt, one strip of tartan looped over his shoulder and fastened with a silver brooch. "Expect that to be the case for the next hundred years or so." Soft words from her mate, along with another toe-curling nuzzle. "Do we have an understanding, my sweet water nymph?"

"Aye, we do, and I will enjoy every moment of it." She swished her skirts, the intricately woven red fabric adorned with embroidery around the hem, a black fur-lined cape secured at her neck, her leather boots laced tightly to her knees, footwear Flora had oohed and aahed over when they'd joined her and Cherub and Kirk in the private dining room for breakfast, the table set only for the five of them.

Wanting to gift Flora with an identical pair of boots, she'd waved Flora's fluffy slippers away and replaced them with the same footwear as her own, and Flora had beamed and hugged her.

Their morning meal, only a short time later, had come to an end far sooner than any of them had wished, but time was of the essence, their task set. Since Calder had been to Triton's lair, all they needed to do was find him at the Druid Pool and ask him to take them there, which might be far faster than interviewing each of Flora's kin about the amulet. A fact they'd all agreed with.

"At least the weather is on our side." Firm words from Kirk as he joined them.

"Aye, I'm grateful there's no rain in sight." She was more than grateful. "Making our way into the mountains would've been far more difficult if I had a tail."

"We could've popped you in a wheelbarrow and carted you about." Smiling, Cherub stepped across the threshold at the front door of Dunvegan, her royal blue velvet skirts peeking through the folds of her hooded fur cloak, a delicate silver chain-link belt skimming her hips and her sparkly skin hidden other than for a peek of her nose and cheeks. Sneaking a furtive glance at the camera over the front door, the lens slowly sweeping toward the curtain wall, Cherub continued, "'Tis a shame they rerecord over the security footage every twenty-four hours. I would have liked to have viewed the recording from the night Flora saw the selkies."

"She's asked the security team to extend all future recordings." Kirk palmed the hilt of his sword holstered at his side, the hem of his black tunic fluttering over his dark pants. Eyeing Lilias, he asked, "Could you telepath Ailith and see if she has any wise words to offer us before we make the trek to the Druid Pool?"

"Of course." Swiftly, she reached out along the pathway to her sister's mind, then added Levi, Cherub, and Kirk to her connection. *"Sister, we're all here at Dunvegan Castle."*

"Your timing is impeccable, Lilias. I've just had a vision this morn and spoken to Murdock about it." Excitement shimmered in Ailith's voice. *"He has seen what I've seen, and together we've received enough impressions to know you're at a turning point. First, I caught sight of our water fae. Shaw, along with Devon, have used the pulley system to remove all of the largest of the boulders, but now they need Cherub and Kirk's aid to uncover the rest of our seabed portal."*

"But we're about to leave for the Druid Pool," Cherub uttered to Ailith with a frown. *"Are you certain Shaw and the seabed portal cannae wait?"*

"Aye, I'm certain. You and Kirk must return to our fae realm. Shaw needs you to open one of your own portals from the safety of the shore of Loch Heart all the way down to the debris covering our seabed portal. If you can funnel the smaller rocks into your portal and suck them up to the shore, then the water fae will have their gateway portal back. An absolute necessity. Shaw said the idea was yours."

"'Twas," Cherub confirmed. *"Although opening a*

portal underneath the sea is something I've never attempted afore. There are so many variables to consider, undersea currents, the stirring of sediment, the velocity of wind I need to conjure, and how that wind reacts with the chilly depths of the sea. I'd need to practice away from our gateway portal to ensure I didnae damage it while sucking the stones and debris away. That practice could take a few hours, or mayhap even a day."

"*I have every faith you'll succeed,*" Ailith stated.

"*I dinnae wish to leave Lilias.*" Cherub growled under her breath.

"*I understand, but Flora didnae have an image of the Druid Pool, only a rudimentary map, so getting there must be done by foot. Lilias and Levi can make that trek, and once they reach the Druid Pool, Lilias can telepath you an image so you can open a portal and join them. This way, we get two jobs done in the time span of one.*" Ailith cleared her throat. "*Levi, I have further instructions for you during your trek into the mountains. Allow your bear to follow the scent of the stag. The animal will lead you to the highest ground, and in that place, where the grass grows thick, you will find a waterfall, a place beyond where the fairies play, beyond the standing stone marked with moss. 'Tis the place where the ancient of Ancients once dwelled, and in finding that place, you will find Calder. Await his arrival.*"

"*You first mentioned that Lilias and I would sitting before a pool when a water portal opened,*" Levi uttered.

"*Aye, and I believe the Druid pool is that pool,*" Ailith verified. "*I must go, and so must each of you. I shall speak to you again soon.*" Ailith's voice drifted away as she closed the link.

"Kirk and I will aid Shaw at Loch Heart, but you must send me the image of the Druid Pool as soon as possible." Cherub grasped Lilias's hands. "Should you need me sooner, telepath me."

"Aye, of course." Lilias squeezed her aunt's hands in return.

"Kirk," Cherub murmured as she stepped away, "disable the camera under the eaves. I dinnae want our leaving captured on film."

"Will do." He tipped the camera lens down, its focus on the mat under the front door.

"That's perfect." With a swish of one hand, Cherub sent dust and leaves swirling over the cobbles. The wind tunneled and a portal opened. She and Kirk got sucked away into the dark abyss, gone within the blink of an eye, the leaves slowly settling once more.

"We're all on our own for a little while." She cupped Levi's cheek.

"We'll find the stag, find the Druid Pool, then find Calder. Freeing Breena and bringing her home is imperative." Levi flicked the camera back into position with the tip of his blade, sheathed his weapon at his hip and seized her hand. He tugged her toward the forest. "There's no time to tarry."

He guided her out the gate and over the stone bridge, his pace fast.

She hurried along the narrow gravel pathway running parallel to the shoreline of Loch Dunvegan. The water rippled a seamless blue. So much blue, a sublime, peaceful blue.

Breathing in the salty sea air, she walked behind Levi until they reached a divide in the path. He headed inland, and she followed as they left the sea behind and trekked toward the mountains.

"We need to pick up our pace." Levi began to jog, and she followed suit, the two of them moving quickly along the meandering path.

They entered the tree line, the heady fragrance of pines swirling all around, her chosen one's gaze roaming from side to side.

Over the hours that followed, he slowed his pace in some places, sniffed deep, then picked up his pace again as he caught the scent he was after.

"Is it the stag?" she checked as she dipped her head under a low branch sweeping across the trail.

"I've finally got it, and his scent is strong." He rubbed his neck, gave it a squeeze along the spot where his muscles appeared to tense up.

She wanted to rub that spot for him, to help ease whatever troubled him. "Is all well?"

"My bear wants out." Need rang strong in his voice.

"Then release him."

"It's best that I do." He unstrapped his weapons, unbuckled his boots. After releasing his kilt, he let it fall to the bracken and leaves underfoot, then loosened the ties of his white tunic and pulled it over his head. "I usually bring a satchel, dump my clothes in it and swing it onto my back when I'm in bear form."

"I'll fashion one for you." She waved a hand, his effects now encased in a satchel made from thick canvas with leather straps that would fit around his waist. "Will that do?"

"It's perfect. I have a very clever mate." He secured the satchel around his middle and standing tall and strong before her, lifted her off her feet and kissed her.

She kissed him back, deeply and passionately, although far too soon he released her and stepped back.

In a sizzling display of crackling energy and shooting light, he shifted and on his rear legs, nudged her back until she knocked her back against a wide trunk, his claws digging into the rough bark either side of her. Slowly, ever so slowly, he rubbed his furry cheek against her cheek. "*Lilias.*" He spoke her name along their merged link, his husky voice reverberating through her mind. "*My bear wants to eat you.*"

"*He can do that later. Right now, he needs to follow the scent of the stag.*" She ducked out from under one paw. "*Lead the way to the Druid Pool.*"

Dropping down onto all fours, he released a rumble and lumbered deeper into the forest. Sniffing, he tracked the stag's scent, while she followed behind him along the trail edged with low brush and thick grass. Overhead, birds twittered from high in the dark green canopy, and all around, she caught the scurrying sound of small creatures scampering through the thick vegetation. Two red squirrels dashed across the path near her feet, their little ears going up and reddish-brown tails curled as they disappeared into the underbrush on the other side. Up the nearest tree, the cheeky squirrels climbed before peering at her through the branches. Adorable.

Levi had disappeared around the far bend, and she hurried and caught up to him.

Insects buzzed all around them.

The wind breezed through the trees.

The earthy dampness of the soil swirled all about.

Towering pines swayed, the thick trunks and wide boughs creaking.

She hiked onward after her mate, passing through a narrow gorge as the sun rose higher in the sky. Never had she wandered so far from the sea, could in fact no longer even see a dot of blue along the horizon.

Releasing a long breath, she trekked upward, the elevation getting higher, until a few steps ahead Levi suddenly stopped and lifted his nose high in the air.

"Can you sense something?" she asked as she ran her fingers through his soft fur. Caressing between his ears, she smiled as he stretched his neck.

"*I can hear the trickle of water,*" he stated in her mind.

"Where is it coming from?"

"*I'm not sure, but we're about to find out.*" He shifted, all six glorious feet of him, until he stood over her. Gently, he touched his lips to the top of her head, stepped back with a pained grunt, and donned his clothes and weapons.

Done, he marched onward, and they soon found the source of the trickling water. A small stream cut through a gorge between two mountain peaks, the stream shallow, but there all the same. They followed the path, the terrain getting rockier and harder to traverse.

Taking care with each step, she scaled the stony mountain pass where the odd loose rock sheared away and clacked down into the corrie below.

As the sun dipped lower along the horizon, she halted on a side ridge and caught her breath as the heavenly glow of burnt orange and sunset yellow caused shadows to lengthen from the brush, the darkness reaching out like long tentacles toward her in the waning light.

She rubbed her chilled arms under her fur cloak, the coldness of the night seeping into her.

"Are you cold?" Levi circled around her.

"Strangely, I am. An unusual phenomenon for me, particularly when I can tolerate the coldest ocean currents below the sea. But when I've been landbound for too long, cooler temperatures effect me."

"Then we'd best find that Druid Pool so we can make camp and light a fire for the night. I need to ensure you're warm." He set out, and they traversed around the bend and came to an abrupt halt before a cliff face that rose out of nowhere.

"Well, this is unexpected." She placed one palm on the craggy rock wall rising a good twenty feet above her head. To the left and the right of the wall grew thick bushes and tufts of grass. She frowned at Levi. "We've reached a dead end."

"Someone wants us to believe we have." He crouched before the bushes on the left and traced a hoof mark which seemed to disappear through the foliage. Carefully, he separated the branches, pushed through, and vanished completely from her sight.

"Levi!" She rushed after him, the bushes swiftly swallowing her. Skidding on the slick ground, she barely kept her footing as naught but darkness surrounded her. "Where are you?"

"Right here." He caught her around the waist, pulled her up against his hard chest.

"Where are we?" She seized his shoulders and held on as she searched the darkened tunnel, her night vision slowly activating. "Did we enter some kind of stony passageway through the rock wall?

"It appears so. Let's continue on." Taking her hand, he led the way through the tunnel until a dim shaft of light appeared ahead. They emerged through bushes into a clearing lit by the last rays of the setting sun, the rock wall that had blocked their path now standing behind them.

Turning in a slow circle, she squeezed Levi's hand, awe shocking her into silence. This place they'd arrived at appeared like a fantasy. Tiny fairies fluttered all about, some brushing her back and shoulders, others flying overhead, all moving so daintily before sweeping toward an ancient oak tree. Wildflowers waved their bright heads within the clumps of grass, the oak's large roots flowing deep into the earth.

"Look, there." Levi pointed to a stag standing near the far trees with his huge antlers curved and branched, his head held high. With a snort, the stag turned and trod off into the darkness of the night beyond. "We should continue tracking him," he whispered in her ear. "We haven't reached the Druid Pool yet."

"But the fairies..." She stretched out one hand, and one wee creature settled on her palm, so tiny as it lifted its petite face to her, its wings aglow as if dusted by diamonds. Lilias's spirit sang with light, and she twirled around, spellbound by the world they'd entered. Even the night sky appeared magical. Stars appeared one by one, all twinkling within the ebony cloak of darkness above, the moon hanging heavy and full and a vibrant orange in the sky. The fairies danced from one flower to another, their wings beating fast, and the fairy on her palm lifted into the air and fluttered away to join the others.

Levi squeezed her hand. "I can hear the sound of rushing water again. Let's go."

He tugged her into the thick brush of the trees, the stag's hoof marks appearing with a shimmer of golden dust surrounding each mark. So stunning.

Another half hour later, she smiled as the sound of the rushing water got heavier and heavier. Wiping her brow, she climbed a steep pathway of grass and stone then rounded the final corner and passed a standing stone covered in moss. Hand to her heart, she lifted her gaze and caught the heavenly fall of water rushing over a stony mountain precipice and crashing into a large oval pool. A spray misted the air, the trees rimming the edge of the pool glistening dark green under the moonlight.

Such a breathtaking sight.

She licked the mist coating her lips, the water tasting of pure Highland sweetness. Absolutely divine. This pool was made for—

Sparks flared and she toppled over, her boots getting shredded as her tail blasted free.

"Lilias." Levi hunkered down beside her, worry creasing his brow before a slow smile widened his mouth.

"Dinnae laugh at me." She slapped her tail on the grass.

"I can see you're okay. That was a fast Change."

"There is a pool of water." She jabbed a finger at it. "Would you be so kind as to carry me to it?"

"Aye, a swim is well deserved." He stripped off his

clothes and weapons, dumped them on the grass.

"Hurry, please hurry." She waved her clothing away.

"I'm coming." He scooped her into his arms, bounded over the boulders rimming the pool and dived in.

Heavenly water cascaded over her scales, and she played her fingers through the luxurious silken swell of water, her body humming with pleasure at finally being returned to her element. Popping back up to the surface in his arms, she grinned as the waterfall gushed nearby, white water cascading over the sheer ridge and foaming into the pool.

"We made it, right in time for the full moon." Levi eyed her, his skin slick and wet and gleaming under the moonlight, his eyes blazing shifter bright.

"Do you sense the need to chase me?" She stretched her arms high, arched her back and looped them around his neck as she swished her tail.

"Aye, the need is strong." He dipped his head, covered her mouth with his and kissed her passionately before diving with her below the surface.

She kicked with him, her body going slick as it created the oil that kept her warm within the deep blue. Oh my, this pool was far deeper than it had appeared from the surface. They had to be at least thirty feet down and she couldn't allow Levi to go much farther. She had gills, whereas he did not.

Sweeping her tail with brisk force, she curled her body around his body, pressed her mouth to his and pushed air into his lungs. Breathing for him, she kicked them upward until they broke the surface.

"How'd you do that?" he asked as they bobbed within

the rippling waves. "You put air into my lungs."

"The water fae rarely tell others, but I can breathe for anyone when I'm below the surface. That is the way of our skill."

"How long could I survive with you breathing for me?"

"As long as needed."

"Incredible." He stroked down her sides, over her gills, then around to her bottom. Cupping her rear through her scales, his eyes blazing a hungry mix of molten gold, he bent his head to her neck and suctioned his mouth over her rapidly beating pulse point. His teeth grazed her flesh, his mouth moving back and forth in a mesmerizing way. She couldn't hold back as she pressed her breasts against his chest and rubbed her sensitive nipples against his flesh. "You're so beautiful, Lilias. I want to explore your body, to have you twine yourself around me until there's no end to either of us."

He sank his teeth into her neck and bit down hard.

She screamed, sheer pleasure coursing through her.

"I want to make love to my mate under the full moon." He traced down the front of her tail, to where her core throbbed with heat.

She wanted to separate her legs and let him run his fingers along her lower folds, to feel him thrust his fingers deep inside her and make her shatter. Except she had a damn tail. All the sensation was there, all hidden behind the muscle and sinew of her scaly appendage. A cursed appendage she adored yet also wished when she could control the timing of.

Thrusting away from Levi, she splashed to the edge of

the pool, clawed her fingers into a boulder and tried to drag herself up. She slipped back down, hot tears streaking down her cheeks.

"Are you crying?" He lifted her onto the boulder, and water sluiced down her body as he planted his hands on the rock and launched himself out. Crouching beside her, he wiped her tears away.

"I dinnae know why, but if I can cry this easily..." More tears fell, and she scrubbed them away. "Then so can Breena. If she gives into Triton, I'll remain this way forever."

"We'll find Breena. We'll make certain we do. Ailith's visions have been guiding us thus far, and they'll continue to do so." He wrapped his warm hands around her waist and lifted her from the boulder, his biceps bulging and a fierce yet tender look crossing his face. Striding across the grass, the mist of the waterfall still drifting their way, he growled under his breath as he searched for a dry spot.

"Over there." She pointed to the trees thankfully upwind of the spray.

Levi stalked across, and she waved a hand, fashioned a thick woolen blanket, and settled it on the ground.

"Can you whistle us up some towels too?"

"Of course." Another wave and 'twas done, the towels appearing in a pile. Levi laid her down and patted her body dry with a towel, while she used her skill to churn the breeze by manipulating the water molecules within it. The breeze blew and fluttered her hair.

Her mate continued to rub her as he smoothed the towel carefully over her scales so as not to snag the cotton on them. Gently, he roamed up and around her midriff, over her back then dabbed across her breasts and up her neck. Lastly, lifting her hair from her nape, he dried her locks.

"Dry yourself too." She stirred the wind until it blew stronger.

"Will do." Levi stood over her, his legs planted wide as he rubbed his strong thighs and muscled legs. He swept the towel over his arms and across his chest then scrubbed his hair, while she pushed up onto her elbows and seized his calf.

With her fingers curling into his warm flesh, she looked up and up and up. He had such long, powerful legs, the hair springy and thickening where it met the apex of his groin. His balls had pulled tight, his cock straining upward, the length rising to an impressive height. Twin ropes of muscle coursed down his sides, his abdominal muscles cutting across his middle. A hot flush of heat coursed through her. "Come closer," she whispered, her voice thick with need.

"Is this close enough?" He dropped onto the blanket beside her.

"Almost." She smoothed her hand along his jaw, his stubble a sensual tickle under her fingertips, his hair completely dry, the wind fluttering the silky dark strands all about. Her nipples tightened, her need for him intensifying. She wanted her chosen one with a fierceness she could barely hold on to. Raw hunger flowed through her, and she glared at her scales. "Why do I still have a tail? I'm dry."

Her heart dropped as the truth roared through her mind.

"Breena," she whispered. "Triton has her tears."

Such pain blasted within her chest. Too much pain.

Chapter 14

Levi's worst nightmare had unfolded, his mate no longer able to walk on land. Under the heavy orb of the full moon, Levi paced back and forth while Lilias stared up at the night sky on her back with an agonized frown. "Triton might have Breena's tears," he muttered as he returned to her, "but we'll find a way to get them back. We're not letting him take control of the water fae."

"Levi, I see no sign of Calder, nor do we have the amulet, and now we're out of time." She gripped his ankle. "What do we do?"

"We're here at the Druid Pool, right where Ailith said we needed to be." He lowered down to one knee, pointed at the pool. "Have faith in her. Remember her first vision, when she saw the two of us sitting on a boulder beside the pool, you with a tail. That's the pool she saw, and this is where we need to be."

"Aye, I believe that too."

"Seers always see the truth, which means we have to

continue waiting until what your sister has seen unfolds." He stroked over her hip, his desire for her thrumming strongly through him, the full moon pushing his need to the brink. Softly, he ran his thumb across her warm lips, and she squeezed her eyes shut. "Look at me, Lilias."

She opened her eyes, tears welling in the corners.

"We'll find Breena and free her. I give you my word we will."

"I'm sad because I can sense your need through our bond, a need which I feel just as strongly as you do. I want your hands on me. I want you to touch me, to not be repelled by my tail."

"Your tail is stunning, would never repel me. We're going to make love tonight, tail or not. I intend on touching you, bringing you pleasure, and making you soar to the heights of ecstasy." That's what he needed to do, desperately, to know she was with him in this moment and not allowing her frustration and worry to send her thoughts skittering elsewhere. This was their night, the first full moon they'd celebrate as a mated pair. Gently, he touched the corners of her lips and she smiled, then sucked his fingers right into her mouth. "That's better."

"I'm all yours, Levi." She drew in a staggered breath. "I love you."

His heart kicked out of rhythm, her declaration making his chest burst. "I love you more," he managed to say.

"Nay, I love you more." She curled her hand around his nape. "Dinnae make me argue with you on that point."

"You've always loved a good argument, and I'm going to enjoy exploring your body, particularly your sparkly tail." He moved down her curvy form, lifted her lower fin and stroked the glittery webbing, then massaged higher, over her tail and up her sides. He kneaded into her flesh with steady strokes before massaging along the line between her legs. Under the sinew of her tail, he could feel her land legs just below the surface. It was as if both parts of her existed, her tail simply hiding the glorious length of her legs underneath. "Rest and relax while I rediscover my mate's body."

"I'll try, but 'tis hard to lie still when you're touching me so." She rested back, her red locks blowing in the breeze, her breasts a feast he wanted to devour. First though, he wanted to continue exploring her tail. Gliding his hands along the place where he could sense the apex of her groin, he found a slit and slipped his hand inside. She gasped, shoved her elbows behind her and gaped. "Levi?"

"I said relax." He cupped her mound, and she got a whole lot breathless. "Did you know this slit was here?"

"Of course. The merpeople can copulate with or without their tail."

"How interesting." He found her inner folds and slid two fingers deep inside her, her warmth washing over his fingers, then he withdrew and stroked his thumb over her nub.

"Goodness." She fell back, her breasts bobbing about. "I've never…I've never…"

"I've never done it this way either, but we're about to make love with your tail." Grinning, he parted her slit wider, added a third finger and plunged even deeper inside her. She bucked, her back arching off the blanket, her inner channel contracting and pulling his fingers in, her nipples hardening into tight points. "I see you like that, my sweet water nymph."

"I adore your touch no matter what form I take."

"Are you ready for more?" At her breathy nod, he stroked her harder, faster, caressing his thumb across her nub in tight circles until she arched even more into his touch.

"Levi, I need you inside me."

"Soon. I have a desire to taste you first." He dipped his head and speared his tongue through her slit and swept into her channel. Licking her flesh, he took her to the edge with his mouth in the most intimate way. His cock got rock hard and dripped from the head. Keeping up his rhythm, the taste of her an aphrodisiac on his tongue, he stroked back and forth until a fiery heat sizzled at the base of his spine, the sensation of need building higher and higher until he had nowhere to go other than to push his cock inside her.

"Levi, have mercy," she whispered raggedly.

"I'm coming, my love." He seized his cock and unable to hold back a moment longer, thrust himself between her slit and went balls-deep inside her. Stars burst behind his closed eyelids. So much pleasure. Too much pleasure. Hands gripping her hips, he covered her mouth with his and kissed her until she whimpered and arched into him. Pounding harder and deeper, Levi lost his mind as her inner muscles tightened and spasmed around him. Her contractions sent him soaring over the edge and he roared, his release blasting violently along with hers, his seed spurting deep inside her core.

"Oh my." She sighed into his mouth, her hands on his butt as she held him close. "'Tis like all of me is filled with you."

"That seems to be the case." He doubted he'd ever want to leave the incredible heat of her body.

She grinned and kissed the tip of his nose. "We could have a whole school of fish."

"No fish. We're having a litter of cubs." He clamped his mouth on the sensitive skin of her neck and suckled her warm flesh, then he bit down and stamped his mark on her before licking the spot and gliding lower. With his chin brushing the upper swells of her breasts, he nipped and laved all around each globe, her nipples tight peaks of pink. "I haven't asked, but will any children we have hold immortality as you do?"

"Aye, as we both do. Their souls will become entwined with mine as they develop in the womb, their immortality secured in that way. They will be as I am, and as you now are, one of the immortal fae."

"As soon as I sense you're in heat," he murmured as he kissed each of her nipples, lazily and with a razz of his teeth, first one glorious bud and then the other, "then I'll get you with child."

She was his mate. Always his. Whether she swam in the sea or walked on land. He'd never allow anyone or anything to tear them apart, not the threat Triton posed or this glorious tail she now possessed.

He grasped her bottom and kissed her, the two of them rolling across the grass as the full moon shone down on them from high above. 'Twas time to learn even more of her body, every voluptuous inch.

Chapter 15

An owl hooted in the dark and Lilias opened her eyes, the tip of her tail chilled from where it poked out from between Levi's legs. She edged onto her side and smiled as her mate, his big body emitting an enticing heat, smiled in his sleep. Softly, she swept back a lock of his silky dark hair behind his ear. The soft haze of moonlight trickled over the ends of the dark strands and across his chiseled jaw holding a razz of stubble. She couldn't help but touch his broad shoulders, so wide and thick with muscle. Caressing his golden skin, she smoothed down over the brawny indentations of his abdominal muscles. This man was all hers.

Leaning closer, her mouth once more watering for a taste of him, she kissed his shoulder then trailed a path along his neck. Over his throbbing pulse point, she scraped her teeth back and forth and his breathing halted, as if he were awake and awaiting her next move. Likely, he was, so she sucked his skin between her lips and once she'd made a lavish red mark, she sank her teeth deep and giggled as he growled, the sound rumbling from deep within his chest. "Good morn, my adventurous bear."

"One night soon we will sleep in our waterbed," he murmured, his long black lashes lifting, his golden shifter eyes smolderingly hot. "I give you my word we will."

"I think we've made do rather well since arriving on the Isle of Skye. There is a soft cushion of grass beneath me and the dark depths of a pool nearby. That is sheer heaven." Rolling on top of him, she crossed her arms over his chest, her breasts pressed against his deliciously defined pectoral muscles. "I wish to wake up this way every morning, but it'll be daybreak soon and my scales are itchy and dry. I need a dip in the pool."

"I'll come with you, since I've no desire to be separated, not even for a moment."

"Oh, wait." She clutched a hand to her mouth. Since their arrival last eve, she'd been so caught up in her chosen one she'd completely forgotten to telepath Cherub an image of this pool, which would allow her aunt to open a portal to this place and rejoin them as soon as they were able, not that she wanted her aunt here right at this moment, not when she and Levi were still naked.

"Are you thinking about Ailith's vision?"

"Nay, about telepathing Cherub. Doing so completely slipped my mind. I must give her the image of this pool, right after we've swum. First though, I need just a little more time alone with you."

"I could lie here all day provided I had you at my side." Gently, he swept one hand into her hair, palmed the back of her head, and drew her mouth to his. Kissing her, he stroked his other hand down her body before tickling along the scales covering her hips and outer thighs. The night sky lightened further until the dark blue became fused with golden yellow and pale pink.

She rubbed her itchy scales, unable to halt her grimace.

"You're in pain. Let's get you into the water before you dry out any further." He launched to his feet, taking her effortlessly with him. "Do you want to breathe for me again below the surface?" he asked with a wink. "We could dive right to the bottom and explore the depths."

"Aye, I would like to explore the depths since we didnae reach the bed of this pool last eve." She kept ahold of his neck, her arms looped tightly around his nape, her tail brushing the grass as he walked. "First though, could we swim over to the waterfall? I've always enjoyed swimming within the bubbles as they foam."

"One waterfall coming up. I remember my first dip under a waterfall. There are several falls on Matheson land along the mountain range. I'll take you to each of them once we've completed this mission." He carried her onto the boulders edging the pool, the deep, husky rumble of his voice holding an enchantment akin to that which the water held for her. Listening to him speak was as divine as feeling the flow of the water sliding over her body whenever she swam within the deep blue.

She took in the mesmerizing falls lit with a rainbow of colors, from sunrise yellow to azure blue and a bewitching violet. The heavy flow cascaded into the pool and foamed across the surface toward the embankment of boulders they stood upon.

Her mate lowered and settled her atop a wide, flat stone before easing down and sitting behind her, his chest brushing her back and his feet dunked in the water either side of her tail. The flow of water seeped into her lower appendage and rejuvenated her, just as his presence did.

He stroked one hand over her hip, a frown suddenly marring his brow. "Am I imagining it or are your scales changing color?"

She flapped her tail in and out of the water, a sparkle of emerald shimmering within the pearl, the same emerald color as her eyes, while along the very tip of her fin a subtle shade of gold now tinged the webbing. She dunked her tail back under the surface, raised it again. The new colors remained. "Well, how interesting."

"You're evolving."

"The merpeople all have pearl-colored scales."

"Reach out to Shaw. Ask him if his tail just changed color? I'll keep myself amused while you do." He swept her hair away from her neck and sank his teeth deep into her skin. He marked her hard and fast.

Her breath stuttered.

"Everything all right?" Another deep bite.

"Aye, all is well." Settling her head back against his shoulder, she released a soft sigh.

"Ailith said we'd be sitting on a boulder just like this when the water swirled as if a portal was being opened before us." Bending, he scooped a handful of water and allowed it to trickle slowly over her lap, the clear water soaking into her scales, her tail, this morning, absorbing every drop on offer.

"Aye, she did."

The wind suddenly changed and dark clouds swirled overhead, just as they did over Loch Heart when one of the water fae opened the gateway portal far below the sea. A bolt of lightning struck the surface of the pool, and the water churned, washing up onto the rocks and spilling back.

"Levi, I think Ailith's vision is taking form now." Swiftly, she clothed herself in a tunic that covered her breasts and bottom. Next, she waved clothes onto him, a loose white tunic and a belted kilt, while he flicked a hand toward his boots and weapons lying on the grass, the items disappearing and apporting to his side with his skill.

He strapped his sword on and slid one dagger into a leather sheath at his wrist and the other into a sheath at his ankle. With his boots tugged on, he scooped her from the boulder and held her tight as thunder boomed and another bolt of lightning struck the surface.

A huge geyser spurted high, and waves washed out.

From the explosion of water came a man with a tail. Shaw. "Oh my, our gateway portal must be operational again," she uttered in a rush to Levi, "not that it has a sequence that reaches here." Hands to her mouth, she shouted over the wind and thunder. "Come over here, Shaw!"

"Where am I?" he shouted back as he kicked toward her.

"The Druid Pool on the Isle of Skye."

Grasping the boulder, he eyed her with clear confusion. "I didnae expect our seabed portal to bring me here."

"How did you manage it?"

"After we'd cleared the last of the rubble with Cherub's aid, I found a new symbol previously hidden by the sand and stone. I pressed that symbol and the chevron locked into place. A huge funnel of water sucked me into the portal afore I could move to a safer distance. The portal spat me out here."

"What did the symbol look like?"

"'Twas a Celtic circle with a large pearl embedded in the center."

"That's the same design as the amulet. Put me back down, Levi." She desperately wanted to speak more to her kin.

"I'm glad you've arrived safely." Levi lowered her back onto the boulder before extending a hand to Shaw and pulling him up onto the slick, rocky surface beside her. "Your tail has changed color too, Shaw. It's the same as Lilias's."

"Cherub was the first to notice the change in color just afore dawn. We've all, each of the water fae, lost our ability to gain our land legs." He slicked his hair back, gave Levi a nod of thanks, then eyed Lilias. "I've never seen that symbol on any of the other seabed arches across the realms. Have you?"

"Nay, but it has brought you here to the Druid Pool, a sacred place that once belonged to the ancient of Ancients, the Tuath Dé, and we both know that our race and theirs were once rather closely aligned." She rubbed her scales, her need to dunk herself fully in the pool overwhelming her. "Mayhap the Tuath Dé added the symbol to our seabed portal so we could remain connected to their Druid Pool."

"That seems a logical explanation, although it

would've helped if they'd told us about it." Shaw scratched his scales. "I've got to get back into the water. The itch is strong."

"I'll come with you." She slid into the water with him, dunked herself under and came back up. "It might take us some time to get used to that itch."

Another clap of thunder boomed, and more lightning sizzled across the sky. The water churned stronger within the pool, a whirlpool forming and growing wider and wider. Within a fizz of bubbles, a woman emerged, her tail swishing under the surface as she scooped the water at her sides.

"Ula?" Lilias swam to her. "Did you come through our fae seabed portal too?"

"Nay, I have no' been to your realm, but instead been trying to reach you, have traveled by way of my amulet." Ula grasped the charm swaying from a chain at her neck, the large Celtic circle adorned with a pearl in the center. "Breena asked me to find you and I needed my amulet for that task, except when I called forth your name, a whirlpool portal took me to No Man's Sea, the in between place. I've never told another, but there is one stipulation when using the amulet. One cannae wish their way to whomever they desire when that person is currently desired more strongly by another. The last time it happened, I got trapped in No Man's Sea after using the amulet to wish my way to Mary, one of my sister sirens, although Mary had been honeymooning with her human lover at the time, and only once Mary dived into the water without her lover, did the whirlpool return and allow me to travel to her. I had to wait three days in between the realms, but this time just over a day. I would have come sooner if I could've."

"I've been with my mate. Meet Levi Matheson, one of the shifter-fae from Matheson Castle. We've been inseparable until mere moments ago when I slipped into the water without him."

"'Tis a pleasure to meet you, Levi." Ula raised a hand to him.

"I'm rather thankful you're here." Levi crouched on the rock, his sword catching the rays of the rising sun. "You must tell us about Breena."

"Aye, you must." Lilias needed to keep her mind focused on saving her kin. "Breena must have given Triton her tears late last eve since that is the time when Shaw and I lost our land legs." She gestured to her fae kin. "Shaw just arrived from the fae realm."

"This is all my fault," Ula uttered. "I should have tried harder to free Breena. She's being kept in a cage deep inside Triton's lair, the lock unbreakable. You can use my amulet to reach her, but you must take reinforcements with you."

"I'll telepath Cherub and Kirk."

"Aye, you'll need Cherub's strong skill." Ula swished her hands at her sides, the water rippling. "Breena said the spell Triton spoke over her and your water fae is one that's linked to his life, so if you wish to gain your land legs back then you must do two things. Retrieve Breena's tears, then make certain Triton's spell is broken by ensuring he ceases to breathe."

"Ula!" A man emerged along the ledge from behind the veil of the falls attired in full warrior clothing, combat leathers and a sword gleaming in a baldric across his back.

He jogged from the ledge onto the boulders, his voice catching as he lowered to one knee and caught Ula's hand as Ula reached him along the embankment. "Is all well, my love?"

"Calder, Breena's been captured by Triton."

"What the hell is he up to now?" Calder scooped Ula from the water and held her tight in his arms, her tail sweeping down.

"He wishes to transfer his curse to another of his tailed kind."

"What curse?"

"Poseidon punished him for trying to take Atlantis away from King Atlas, his curse locking his land legs away for a hundred years, except Triton found a way to circumvent it. He's already captured Breena's tears, the curse transferred to her and her fellow water fae. That's why I'm here. I needed to give Lilias my amulet so she can rescue Breena, my charm bringing me by way of a whirlpool to your Druid Pool."

"Damn the man. Triton's devious and unscrupulous, will never change." Calder canted his head toward Lilias in the pool. "You must be Lilias?"

"Aye, Levi and I came in search of you." She scooped water at her sides. "We've spoken to your daughter, are aware of your heritage and hers."

"She clearly placed her trust in you." Calder cast a look at Levi, his frown deepening. "I didn't expect to see you here, Levi. How are you involved in all of this?"

"I'm mated to Lilias." Levi crossed to Calder, grasped his shoulder, and explained all that he could, catching Calder up as quickly as possible without missing any vital information.

"I see," Calder uttered afterward, his dark hair sweeping about his shoulders in the wind. "As one of the Druids of the Isle of Skye, I've always guarded this sacred place, ever since the ancient of Ancients left the mortal world for the Otherworld. As the guardian of the Druid Pool, 'tis my duty to give aid to those on Earth who need it. Is there aught you have need of?"

"No, not now Ula has arrived with her amulet," Levi answered him.

"Please, take it." Ula removed the Celtic treasure and passed it to Levi. "'Tis yours and Lilias's for as long as you need it."

"Thank you." Levi lowered to a crouch, held it out to Lilias in the water. "Take it."

"I'll look after it, Ula, will return it as soon as we've freed Breena." She accepted the amulet from Levi and slid the necklace over her head, then opened a link to her aunt and sent the image of the Druid Pool to her. 'Twas time to leave for Triton's lair. No more could they delay.

Chapter 16

"Can you give us more information on Triton's lair?" Levi asked Ula as he bounded into the water and joined Lilias.

"There's a large pool inside his underground cavern, more than sufficient for a whirlpool to form. There are also streams of air within the whirlpool's portal for those who cannae breathe below the surface as the merpeople can, but beware, Triton has been trying to get his hands on my amulet for centuries. He knows what it can do."

"We'll take all care." Overhead, Levi braced himself as lightning sizzled and the dark clouds got even darker, the wind howling all around.

"Cherub comes," Lilias called over the gust.

More wind, the grass flattening, then a portal opened near the trees and Cherub and Kirk stepped free of the vortex, the wind of Cherub's portal slowly subsiding. She and Kirk raced across the grass, bounded onto the boulders, and dove into the pool. They joined him and Lilias, Cherub hugging her niece before pulling back, her hands on Lilias's shoulders. "You have the amulet, my dear niece. Good work."

"I've got it, except we're running out of time. I've lost my land legs." Lilias gestured to her tail.

"I'm aware. All of the water fae are the same." Frowning, Cherub cast her gaze to Shaw. "Here you are. We all wondered where that new symbol took you."

"It appears we now have a direct portal to this Druid Pool," Shaw confirmed.

"I need you to return through it and inform the water fae that we're leaving to find Breena now. We willnae return without her. Tell them they have my word."

"Will do, and take care, all of you." Shaw dived and kicked down deep, his form disappearing into the murky dark below the surface.

Lilias grasped the amulet. "Everyone, hold onto me and remember, dinnae fight the pull of the whirlpool."

"We willnae let go." Cherub seized Lilias's outstretched hand, Kirk taking her other hand, while Levi wrapped an arm around his mate's middle from behind.

"We must be prepared for a battle upon our

arrival." As soon as Levi sighted Triton, he'd release his beast and let him ravage the man. He would ensure Triton paid for his crimes against Lilias's water fae. "I demand first clawing."

"I'll take the second." Fur rippled across Kirk's forearms.

"It's time to go." Placing one hand over Lilias's hand on the amulet, he focused on Breena and added his wish to his mate's, that they would be taken by the whirlpool directly to Breena.

A screech of wind tore through, the sky overhead getting blacker, heavier, the treetops surrounding the pool bending and bowing, his mate having activated the charm with their combined wishes. Leaves and clumps of grass blew everywhere, the water surging in waves that slapped the surrounding embankment of boulders. A whirlpool suddenly opened and together, they were yanked and pulled into the churning swirl and sucked below the surface.

Through the dark they rode the waves of water and wind, the churning abyss similar to Cherub's portals. He pulled Lilias closer, dipped his head and clamped his teeth on the sensitive skin of her neck. He could breathe easily within the streams of wind, just as Cherub and Kirk could too, the water slapping into them here and there.

Tunneling deep into his mate's mind, he opened the private pathway that would always belong to them, and their link shone with vibrant life, brilliant golden filaments lining each side of it. Growling deep in his chest, he tucked his mouth against the other side of her neck and bit her there too before murmuring along their link, *"We battle together, my sweet water nymph."*

"Aye, always." Lilias pointed ahead to where a yellow light glowed. *"We're almost there."*

They broke through the light and kicked free of the portal into an underwater cavern with steam hissing off black rock walls and water lapping against black sand. A cage sat half-submerged, the door clanking back and forth with the waves, the cell empty.

Levi searched the cavern. Up ahead, several lit torches were staked into the sand leading toward a passageway. He breathed deep, caught two distinct scents in the air, one masculine and one feminine. Surging through the water, he called back to Kirk, "Triton is on the move with Breena."

"He must have seen the whirlpool form in the cavern and understood the hunt was on." Kirk pounded after him.

Levi bounded onto the sand and crouched next to a set of fresh footprints. They measured the same foot size as his own, the prints embedded deep and giving proof Triton must be carrying Breena in her tailed form. "Why take her with him?"

"To use as leverage. That's what I'd do in his case." Kirk crouched next to him, water dripping from his hair onto the sand.

Over his shoulder, Levi caught Lilias bobbing in the water, one hand clutching the amulet at her neck, her expression grave. "Have you got your pouch of fae dust?"

"I always keep it close, the dust spelled to remain dry." She swung the pouch from one wrist.

"Then we'll use it to outwit him." He rose to his feet, nodded at her. "Use your dust to forge a replica of the amulet."

She arched an intrigued brow. "Aye, I shall."

"Let me lift you out of the water first," Cherub offered as she rose, one arm looped around Lilias's arm, the two floating higher until they cleared the water.

After pinching a little dust, Lilias sprinkled it over Ula's amulet and murmured the words, "Where there is one, now let there be two." A second amulet shimmered forth, identical in every way to the original. Lilias removed Ula's amulet from around her neck and slipped it inside her pouch, leaving the replica at her neck. His mate gestured toward the passageway where the prints led. "Let the hunt begin. Cherub and I will be right behind you."

"Keep up." Racing along the tunnel, the sand giving way to firm rock under his feet, he kept a fast pace with Kirk a mere step behind. A hundred feet on, the passageway ended, the opening spewing out onto a rocky ledge, and he skidded to a stop. Along the horizon, the rising sun glowed, the golden-pink rays spearing into the pale blue of the new day, the sea rippling for as far as the eye could see, while below, waves splashed against the beach and foamed up onto the sand.

"Oh my." Cherub whooshed in beside him and Kirk, her gaze widening on the sheer drop of the cliff face. "Triton must have used a spell to float himself down. Kirk, Levi, take ahold of me. I'll settle us all down on the beach."

He did as commanded, his fingers brushing Lilias's fingers curled around Cherub's arm, Kirk grasping Cherub's hips as their fae princess lifted the four of them over the edge and whisked them down to the beach. Once she'd dropped them onto the sand, she lifted back up with his mate so her tail didn't scrape the sand.

Levi searched for more footprints.

"Over there by the dunes." Lilias flapped her tail, her skin and scales dry from the sea breeze, her long red locks fluttering about her waist. "I've got a higher vantage point, and I see footprints."

"Good spotting." Levi gritted his teeth and jogged after Kirk who'd already taken off.

Triton's footprints disappeared over the sandy rise of the dunes.

Drawing in a deep breath, Levi tried to catch the scent of his prey, except only a trace of it scented the air. Onward, he ran. He bounded over spiky tufts of grass, the sea crashing into the shore on his left and the grass growing thicker on his right.

"Look, it's Oadh and Roy," Cherub called as she pointed out at sea toward two massive seals surging from the waves. The seals clambered onto the sand and rose onto their hind flippers, their nostrils flaring and whiskers moving. Oadh and Roy shook, their skins rippling down to their waists. "Oadh, Roy, meet Levi and Kirk," Cherub whispered in a rush. "What brings you here?"

"Our mother sent us." Oadh tossed Levi a skin he pulled out of a pouch strapped around his middle. "Two nights past, Aisling sent us to Dunvegan Castle to retrieve our half-brother's skin. She foresaw that ye would have need of it in yer coming battle with Triton. Return it to Calder when ye are done."

"Did she also send you to steal Ula's amulet from Dunvegan Castle?" Levi asked Oadh. "Flora said she saw two seals in the loch the night before it went missing, although she didn't say it was you."

"Aye, 'twas us, and 'tis been over a century since we last saw Flora, no' that we've ever spent a great deal of time with her." Remorse lurked in his eyes. "Our mother foresaw that the amulet must be taken away afore it could once more be found, so we had to travel back in time by a few days and sneak onto MacLeod land."

"Did you do so after we spoke in the Adonis Isles?" Lilias quizzed him.

"Aye, for after we told ye of our mother's vision,

she *saw* further difficulties ahead for ye. Flora almost caught us that night, so we waited until the next day and snuck it off one of the bairns as they swam, then we swam deeper into the channel and left the amulet where our mother told us to, where Ula would find it. We didnae wish to act so underhanded, but all must be carried out as our mother foresees."

"And, exactly, what does she foresee me doing with this skin?" Levi ran his hand over the thick yet velvety soft seal fur.

"When ye need to take to the water, make use of it, the same way all selkies do." Oadh and Roy tucked their skins over their heads and splashed back into the waves. The two of them dived and disappeared below the surface, leaving just as quickly as they'd come.

"They're helpful, aren't they?" A frustrated mutter as he eyed Kirk. "Do you think I should use it?"

"Aisling's a powerful seer, so aye, you should use it. Let's go. We have a madman to catch." Kirk took off toward the headland where Triton's footprints led.

Levi made chase, Cherub and Lilias soaring through the air above.

Aye, they had a madman to catch, and he wouldn't hesitate to slit the man's throat once he had him in hand.

Chapter 17

Lilias held tight to Cherub as her aunt flew over the dunes toward the headland. Below, Levi and Kirk crested the highest dune and skidded down the other side toward an outcropping of boulders where a large tunnel entrance came into sight between two rocky mounds. Her mate and Kirk disappeared inside, and she and Cherub glided down and bobbed along the stone passageway, the gritty rock floor coated in sand and the ceiling thankfully high. The light diminished as they left the entrance behind and her sight adjusted, just as it always did when she swam in the deep blue, but still, to aid Cherub, she pinched some dust from her pouch and whispered a spell that brought forth a torch with a flickering flame. "Take this." She handed it to her aunt.

"You have my thanks." Holding the torch high,

Cherub swished down the winding tunnel leading deeper and deeper into the earth. So deep. Too deep. The air got hotter, muggier, more humid. Cherub rounded the bend just as the men scrambled down a chute. They slipped and slid, unable to keep their footing, while she and Cherub whooshed down behind them.

Along the rock walls, fragments of stone glowed a vivid red, bits seeping through and turning black. Lava? The heat made her gag, the temperature rising with each breath she took. It seared her throat and burned her nostrils. "How much deeper does Triton intend to run?"

"He's devising a strategy, will only halt when he's ready." Cherub narrowed her eyes. "We must be prepared for anything."

"Triton's scent is becoming stronger, Breena's too. Keep up!" Kirk called over his shoulder before he came to a stumbling stop at a divide in the passageway, the tunnel to the right emitting heat and the tunnel to the left wafting with a cool breeze. "We go left," Kirk confirmed.

Both men ducked along the offshoot tunnel and within twenty feet, reached an opening into a massive chamber with cool black water running through it.

Lilias and Cherub joined them, the light from the torch illuminating the massive boulders and high vaulted ceiling that held an array of vivid blue lights. Nay, not lights. Glowworms.

"'Tis a grotto." Cherub breezed across the pool and lowered her down into the water. "Is that better, Lilias?"

"Aye 'tis perfect." Scooping the seawater at her sides, she swam toward Levi as he stripped off his clothes and slid into Calder's selkie skin.

"There's water, so now seems the right time to don this skin." He drew the skin up to his waist, his gaze on the ceiling where stalactites hung, then he eyed each wall and darkened corner of the cavern.

The water tugged at her tail, a slow pull. She dived and found an underwater tunnel below, the pool leading deeper downward. Surfacing back in the cavern, she called out, "Triton's taken Breena through the tunnel system below us, all of it underwater, so we can either dive and I'll breathe for everyone, or we take a whirlpool portal that has an air current streaming through it."

"We can't give him any more time to consider his next move." Levi shuffled closer to the edge of the pool, his gaze direct. "We might have the amulet in our possession, a boon for sure, but he's a sorcerer who can spell. We need to open a whirlpool portal and end this."

"I agree with Levi." Cherub dropped into the pool and seized Lilias's arm. "Triton's time for running is done. We'll deal with him now, once and for all."

"I'm in agreement. We go straight to the source." Kirk bounded in, caught her other arm. "Breena needs us."

"Activate the amulet now." Levi pulled the skin up over his shoulders, shoved his arms into the fore flippers and ducked his head into the seal's head. His golden shifter eyes glowed from the eye sockets, the selkie skin sealing fully around his neck and down his chest, the pelt becoming him. With a rough and husky bark, he slid over the edge of the rocky pool and glided below the water's surface before swimming in a circle, one flipper curling around her belly as he surfaced, his voice firm in her mind. *"I'm ready when you are."*

With one hand on the amulet tucked securely away in her pouch, she uttered the words, "I wish for us to be taken to Breena and Triton."

The water swirled into a whirlpool.

It pulled at her, dragged her and the others down.

Streams of air swished past as the portal sucked them under and sent them spinning away through the dark depths of the sea. She cartwheeled, the streams twisting her around and she lost Cherub and Kirk before catching Levi's hand and holding onto him tight. A yellow light glowed up ahead and as she neared it, the portal thrust her away from her mate, the waves washing her to the surface near the shore, and there, she spied Breena lying face down on the sand, motionless, her tail in the surf where it foamed around her fin. Triton stood over her on his land legs, his body dry as he heaved his trident high. With his gaze narrowed on Lilias, he struck the earth, and a huge wave crashed into her from behind and sent her tumbling toward him.

She rolled onto the sand at his feet, tried to get to Breena, but he slammed his trident down a second time and the earth shook.

"I'm the son of Poseidon, and I will rule over the water fae. Give me Ula's amulet." Another slam of his trident, the rod piercing through her side into the sand. He had her pinned, unable to move. "You will never win a fight against me, Lilias!" His voice boomed with vicious depth. "I knew you'd come for Breena."

"I'll never let you take the water fae as your own." She yanked on the rod, blood bubbling from her mouth. "I forbid it."

"You forbid it?" He broke out into an evil laugh, then waved one hand in the air and spoke a spell that had the imitation amulet around her neck shimmering away and reappearing in his hand. "I shall enjoy bringing you to heel."

A massive seal surged out of the waves. Levi. He burst free of Calder's skin and in a flare of bright sparks his bear roared forth. Her mate came down hard on Triton, his claws digging into his flesh, his teeth shredding Triton's neck until the bones cracked. Snarling and snapping within his bear, her mate continued to claw and kill even though Triton no longer breathed.

"Levi, he's dead! He's dead!" She heaved the trident from her side, blood spurting then dying away to a trickle as her skin healed and sealed over. She belly-crawled toward Levi as he lifted his muzzle and roared over Triton. "He's dead. He cannae harm me anymore."

Levi shifted back in a blast of sparks, his golden eyes blazing. "As soon as he heals, I'm going to kill him again. Don't tell me I can't. No one harms my mate and gets away with it."

"We need to check on Breena."

"We will, right after I've found her tears. Triton must have them on him somewhere." He shoved Triton over, a glass vial swaying from a chain around his bloodied and broken neck, the vial half shattered and liquid dripping onto the sand. Levi yanked the chain fully off and crushed what remained of the vial in his hand, shards of glass cutting into his clenched fist and the last of Breena's tears flowing free between his fingers. "It's done."

"Aye, 'tis done." Relief flooded through her. "Now take me to Breena."

"Of course." He swept her up into his arms and carried her across to Breena, then gently, carefully, set her down next to her friend. "I can see the pulse beating in her neck, so she's definitely breathing," he confirmed.

"So can I, but I dinnae know what he did to her to cause her unconsciousness." She ran her hands up and down Breena's body and checked for any injuries, although if her friend had suffered from any, then her immortal blood had already healed her.

"Your tail, Lilias." Levi stared at it. "Look."

Sparks flared along the entire length of her wet tail, her lower fin tingling.

"Levi, you released Breena's tears," she murmured as she patted her scales, "and by killing him you also released the spell that tied us to him." More sparks, so dazzlingly bright, then her tail shimmered and disappeared, her land legs reappearing just as Breena's did too. Across the sand, Triton's tail flashed back to full and vibrant life, his curse returning to him. "You did it. You freed the water fae from his rule."

"Not just me, all four of us did." He stared out over the water, hands on his hips and a frown marring his brow. "Or maybe just the two of us. At what point did we lose Cherub and Kirk?"

"Somewhere in the whirlpool." She followed his gaze and spied the spot where the water still churned in a strong whirling motion. "The whirlpool is still open. I've got the true amulet in my pouch. I'd better fetch them." Pushing to her feet, she flicked one hand and fashioned a pair of breeches for Levi and soft tunics for her and Breena that reached their knees. "Will you watch over Breena while I'm gone? I don't want her to fret when she awakens."

"How about you stay, and I'll fetch Cherub and Kirk? Calder's skin is incredible to wear. I wouldn't mind putting it on again." He collected the skin from the wet sand and shook it out.

"Wait." She grabbed his arm just as out at sea, Cherub and Kirk broke free of the swirling water and kicked toward them. "Where did you get too?" she yelled to her aunt.

"We lost our hold on you, but thankfully remained in the portal. It took us longer to get through it without you." Cherub slogged up onto the beach, Kirk one step behind her, the two of them a wet mess. "Is Breena all right? I see Triton is dead, unless he's usually that much of a bloodied and broken mess."

"Aye, Breena's alive and we have our land legs back." She hugged her aunt.

"You found me." Slurred words as Breena groggily opened her eyes from where she lay flat on the sand.

Lilias squealed and dashed to her friend, dropped to her knees, and squeezed Breena tight. "I'm sorry it took so long for us to reach you."

"I'm sorry too." Cherub knelt and joined in their hug. "Are you well?"

"I knew my kin would find me." Breena pulled them both close, the surf washing in and bubbling around their feet. "I see I no longer have a tail, which means someone found my tears and rid Triton of them."

"Levi did." Lilias motioned to her chosen one standing shoulder to shoulder with Kirk. "We've forged a mated bond."

"How wonderful." Breena smiled at him. "Levi,

you have my thanks for dealing with Triton."

"I'd say anytime, but I'd rather you not get kidnapped again." He lowered to one knee beside Breena, ran one hand over her head, her face gaining more color.

"I might have a way to ensure we're rid of Triton forever." Lilias strode across to Triton, pinched some dust from her pouch and sprinkled it over his prone body. "With this wish, I ask that it holds true. Never shall Triton be able to speak another spell over the water fae, nor cause any harm or foul to befall us. And may the curse Poseidon handed down to him remain with him for the full length of his punishment, that Triton will never be able to transfer his curse to another as he has done with us." Sparks glimmered and settled as her wish took a firm hold.

"Wait, I saw his finger twitch." Snorting, Levi swooped in and cracked Triton's neck again.

"You're incorrigible." She laughed and grasped his hand, hauled him away. Over her shoulder, she called to Kirk, "If Triton twitches again—"

"Got it. No need to ask." Kirk grinned as he raised a hand. "I'll keep cracking his neck until you two return."

"Where are we going?" Levi brought their joined hands to his lips and kissed her fingertips, his golden eyes glinting.

"Not far. I just wish to be alone with my mate and offer him my thanks without Triton in my sight." She dashed toward the dunes, crested the rise, and ran down the other side.

"Triton who?" Levi caught up to her, lifted her off her feet and twirled her around.

Never had such peace taken ahold of her.

As he slowly lowered her back down, she slid her hands deep into his hair, pressed her mouth to his neck and marked her chosen one, just as she intended on doing for the rest of her life.

A life that had just begun.

A life filled with enchanted dust and magical spells.

A life where wishes could come true.

Chapter 18

Matheson Castle, three days later, an hour before dawn...

Lilias walked to the edge of the shore where Levi stood with his hands in his pockets, a grim look on his face as he eyed the moonlit waves. The golden glow of the waning moon shimmered across the blackened water, the sea calling to her as the surf rolled into shore and slowly receded back. Lifting the hem of her pale-yellow silk gown, she dipped her toes into the bubbly surf next to her mate. "You look worried, my adventurous bear."

"Not worried, just annoyed I gave Calder back his skin already." He stripped his tunic over his head and tossed it onto a beached log on the dunes. "I now look at the water and want to glide through it like a seal does."

"You can still glide through it with me, albeit without a skin." She stepped into the water, the silken swell caressing her ankles and calves.

"I'll be slower without it." He loosened the ties of his breeches and stepped out of them, tossed them onto the log with his other belongings.

"Too slow to catch me?" With a teasing sway of her hips, she walked backwards into the water. Slowly, she unlaced her gown, pushed the silk from her shoulders and let it flutter into the water. Completely nude, she stepped out of the swirling silk then backed up farther, until the sea reached her waist.

"Never too slow for that." Such love radiated in his beautiful golden shifter eyes. "Come here, my sweet water nymph. It's time for a true kiss between lovers under the sea."

"I'll take us under." Heat built in her core, the desperate need she had to join as one with him flaring strong. She focused on her legs and bright sparks flared.

She'd lost her tail after Levi had disposed of Breena's tears, but not the smattering of scales on her calves. So later that day, along with her fellow water fae, they'd all attempted to shift and been successful.

They'd evolved, become more than what they'd ever been before.

She and her fellow water fae could Change at will.

Such joy had erupted from her and her kin, the

moment sublime.

With another shower of sparks, her legs fully fused together, her tail shimmering into vivid form.

Grinning, she took Levi with her as she fell into the waves, then she splashed her tail back and forth as she dived. *"I will never leave you,"* she whispered into his mind.

"I'll never give you the chance." With his hands on her waist, he kicked along with her, the two of them going deeper and deeper.

Covering his mouth with hers, she breathed for him, and he growled as he held onto her, his claws slicing out and in, fur rippling across his shoulders and down his arms until his fur retracted and left his golden skin glistening under the water.

She tickled her fingers across his flesh, a fire of need sweeping through her body, then she moved her lower body in an undulating motion against his, the depths of the sea silky smooth as the water flowed over her upper body and swept past her tail.

Gloriously cool water swirled all around her.

Bliss. Absolute bliss.

The water caressed her body, as did Levi's hands, his cock rigid and hard as he guided his shaft through the slit in her scales and joined them as one. Bubbles fizzed all about, her mouth on his as he pumped into her, and she soared to the stars with her mate flying right by her side.

Never could she have imagined such a beautiful

joining.

He was hers, and she was his.
Until the end of time.

Bonus Scenes – From the Author

I couldn't end this story without a chance to catch up with Ailith, Cairstine, and Cherub. Read on to see how these three ladies are doing with their mated men. Happy reading.

~Joanne

Ailith & Hunter

Ailith giggled as Hunter chased her down a darkened tunnel made of stone and grit. She skidded around a corner and gasped as steam plumed and wafted about her. She stepped deeper into the warm fog and crunched over white grainy sand. The steam cleared, the depths of a cavern opening before her with a pool of hot, rippling water surrounded by slick black stone walls. Boulders and rocks sat scattered across the sandy curve of the beach. They'd arrived at Faodail, her mate's favorite place deep below the ground on his Matheson clan land. Farther along the curve of sand, the tunnel continued, daylight shimmering through an opening just beyond a rock wall, the salty scent of the sea sweeping through from the opening, this cave located right alongside the shores of Loch Alsh. "I cannae believe we're here, Hunter."

"Aye, and all alone as well." Muted light from the tunnel leading outside gently illuminated the recesses of the cavern. Taking care, he set the lamp on the sand near the wall, then unbelted his sword and daggers and placed them next to the lamp. With his boots kicked off, he prowled toward her, lifted his forest-green tunic over his head and tossed it aside. He had a wickedly broad chest, his muscles gleaming a sun-kissed gold, his torso tapering down to lean hips with roped muscles on each side. He snapped the dome of his dark jeans, pushed the worn denim down his legs and stepped clear of them before halting within a hair's breadth from her, his cock jutting up thick and proudly from a thatch of dark curls springing around the base. "Welcome back to my lair, Goldilocks."

"Are you disrobing for a swim…or mayhap for another reason?" She reached up on her toes, hooked her arms around his neck and kissed him, deeply and sensually, her tongue flicking over his tongue.

"All I can say is, don't expect to be wearing any clothes until we need to return to the keep."

"My sisters and I have been waiting over eight-hundred years for our chosen ones. I dinnae wish to return to the keep until I've been well sated."

"That sounded like a challenge to me." He snagged the ties of her black leather vest, loosened them, and slowly opened the front. As he slid her vest from her shoulders, he looked deep into her eyes. "I adore a challenge."

"I adore my mate." Hands on the hem of her cream tunic, she pulled it over her head and dropped it on top of her discarded vest, then unhooked her sword belt while Hunter worked the fastenings of her black breeches. Her breath came harder and faster, the same as his did.

Lowering to his knees, he slid her boots off and drew the soft leather of her breeches down and off, her underwear going with it. Then he grasped her bare bottom and moaned as he nuzzled her golden curls, his breath whistling hotly against the sensitive skin of her mound. "Perfect. This is exactly where I want to be right now."

Fingers itching to touch more of him, she smoothed over his shoulders and dug her fingers into his skin as he spread her legs wider and, oh my, what a wicked tongue her mate had.

He purred, the gentle hum of his bear vibrating in his chest and rising to escape his lips, his attentive kisses so divine. Water lapped into shore, the swell seductive, just as her mate always was when they were together.

Hunter was her chosen one, the only man she'd ever desire, the only one who'd ever hold her very heart and soul.

Cairstine & Liam

Bright gold sunshine beamed between the two-inch gap in Liam's heavy blue drapes where they hadn't quite been drawn together. The sunlight danced over Cairstine's closed eyelids where she lay curled in front of her mate, her back to his chest and his warmth enveloping her. She opened her eyes, stretched one leg out from under the fur bedcovers into the sliver of light and softly sighed as the ray streaked down her leg and warmed her skin. She would never tire of the sight of being in the sun, or that she could once more eat solid food and walk side by side with her mate. She wanted to pinch herself, to know this moment was real, to never go another day without fully appreciating all her chosen one had gifted her. Smiling, she wriggled her pert backside into Liam's groin. Having him hold her throughout the night had brought such wondrous peace to her soul.

"Cairstine?" Mumbling under his breath, he stretched, his muscled body cocooning hers. "Are you awake?"

"Aye, I am."

"Do you need to feed?" He eased one hand over the gentle curve of her hip, then slid his fingertips into the curls guarding her womanhood below. Dipping one finger between her folds, he stroked her nub and sent an array of delicious sensations flaring out.

The strongest sensation being need.

Need to be as one with him.

To have their bodies fully joined in every conceivable way.

That need roared through her as she rolled over and faced him, lowered her head, and fastened her mouth over his left pec. She sank her teeth deep into the vein running right over his heart and blood surged into her mouth, hurtled over her tongue, and flowed into her body. His divine essence soaked into her, replenishing her, his lifeforce iron-rich and incredibly delectable. *"You are my tasty bear,"* she whispered into his mind.

"Hell, I love it when you take your nourishment directly from me." Wrapping his arms tightly around her, he caressed the lower curve of her back then grasped her bare bottom and hoisted her on top of him, his erect cock sliding deep between her lower folds as he settled her in place.

Still feeding, she sucked and sucked, his manhood getting harder and longer and thicker within her. She rocked over top of him, taking him as deep as she could and when she finished her feed and closed the puncture wound, he bit into her neck and marked her as their shifter kind did with their chosen ones.

So much pleasure.

So much love.

So much devotion.

She wished the same for Lilias and Levi, that they too would have the same incredible bond as she had with her mate.

Cherub & Kirk

Cherub dissolved into the air and swished over the curtain wall and up to her and Kirk's bedchamber on the upper floor of Matheson Castle. Hopefully, her mate hadn't awakened yet this morn, the dawn sun having not long arisen. She'd been quiet enough when she'd left a short time earlier, so as not to disturb him. Without a noise, she slid through the two-inch gap under the windowsill and shimmered into full form before the window, her sapphire silk skirts swishing.

Kirk bounded out of bed and dragged her up against his naked, muscular body. "You snuck out without me. Naughty mate. I've been awake ever since you left."

"I wished to check on Lilias and Levi." She hooked her arms around his neck, his stunning golden eyes rimmed with a glimmer of starburst yellow. "I caught them disappearing below the surface, getting wet and ah…well…doing what mates do when they're in love."

"It's amazing how Lilias and the water fae can now forge tails whenever they desire."

"They have evolved, which is what often happens with our fae abilities. Over time, our skills change and adapt, become stronger and deeper."

"Talking about change." He slowly lowered to one knee, touched his nose to her belly and took a deep breath. He lifted his gaze back to hers, a wicked grin cutting across his face. "My elusive imp, if I'm not mistaken, you're changing, going into heat."

"Are you certain?" She grasped his head as he took another deep breath, then squealed as he surged to his feet and ripped her gown from bodice to hem. The scraps fluttered to the floor as Kirk scooped her up and tossed her onto their bed. She bounced, then he was there on top of her, the fine dark hairs on his chest scraping against her nipples and making them stiffen.

"There isn't a chance I'm wrong. You're in heat." With his bear growling low in his middle, he threaded his fingers deep into her long golden locks. "Which means you're not leaving this chamber until I get you with child."

"You sound rather insistent."

"You haven't seen insistent yet." With a heated look and a hungry smile, he kissed her, deeply and wildly, until their bodies came together in a fierce storm, their combined passion scattering all her thoughts.

All except one.

'Twas time to make a babe of their own.

A child born of their love.

Their next adventure awaited them.

Author's Note

Clan Matheson descends from a twelfth century man called Gilleoin, a man who was believed to have been from the ancient Royal House of Lorne. The name Matheson has been attributed to the Gaelic words Mic Mhathghamhuim which means "Son of the Bear," and the clan chief's arms carry two bears as supporters. In the twelfth century, Clan Matheson settled around the area of Loch Alsh, Loch Carron, and Kintail, and gave their allegiance to clan MacDonald whose chiefs were the Lords of the Isles. Clan Matheson became a large and powerful clan with a force of around two-thousand men, although by the middle of the sixteenth century they'd diminished greatly in size and influence due to the blood feuds raging across the isles at that time. This warring left them to possess less than a third of the original Matheson property on Loch Alsh.

It's time for the whispers to reignite. Clan Matheson are the "Son of the Bear."

This story is woven with as much accuracy to the period and locations as possible, although any mistakes made are mine alone. Please feel free to search for any of my other works. I simply adore strong heroines, and have a ton of fun matching them with their honorable alpha heroes.

The Matheson Brothers Series

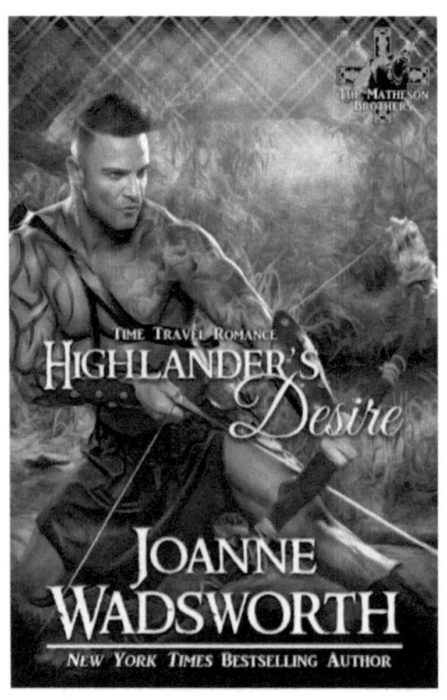

Regency Brides Series

The Duke's Bride, Book 1
The Earl's Bride, Book 2
The Wartime Bride, Book 3
The Earl's Secret Bride, Book 4
The Prince's Bride, Book 5
Her Pirate Prince, Book 6

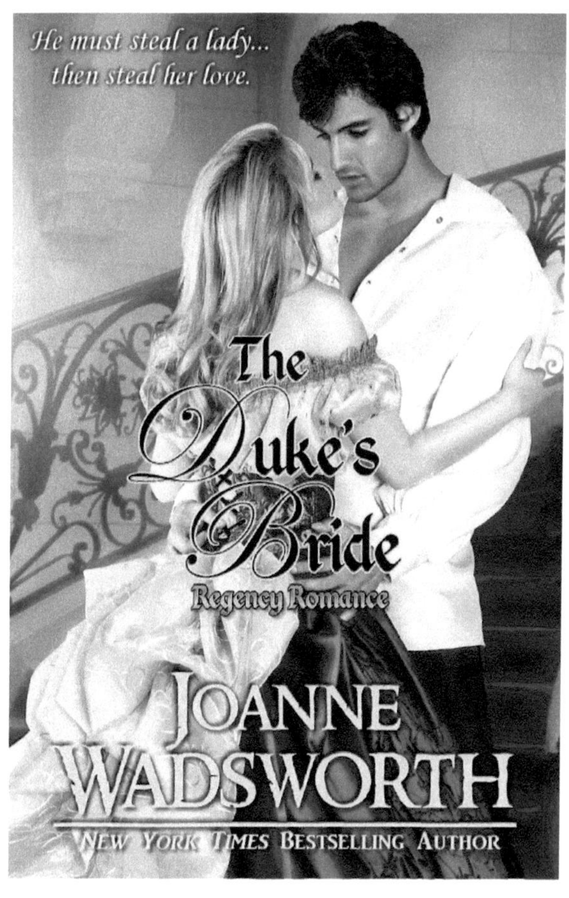

Highlander Heat Series

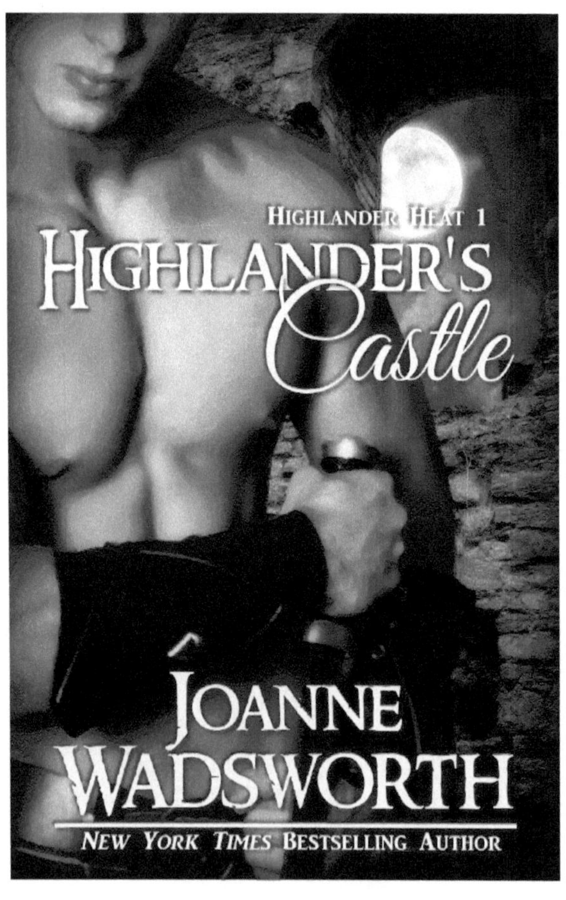

JOANNE WADSWORTH

Joanne Wadsworth is a *New York Times* and *USA Today* Bestselling Author who adores getting lost in the world of romance, no matter what era in time that might be. Hot alpha Highlanders hound her, demanding their stories are told and she's devoted to ensuring they meet their match, whether that be with a feisty lass from the present or far in the past.

Living on a tiny island at the bottom of the world, she calls New Zealand home. Big-dreamer, hoarder of chocolate, and addicted to juicy watermelons since the age of five, she chases after her four energetic children and has her own hunky hubby on the side.

So come and join in all the fun, because this kiwi girl promises to give you her "Hot-Highlander" oath, to bring you a heart-pounding, sexy adventure from the moment you turn the first page. This is where romance meets fantasy and adventure…

To learn more about Joanne and her works, visit
http://www.joannewadsworth.com